Praise for the

"Daley's characters come to life on the page. Her novels are filled with a little mystery and a little romance which makes for a murderous adventure."

– Tonya Kappes,
USA Today Bestselling Author of *Fixin' To Die*

"Daley's mysteries offer as much sizzle and pop as fireworks on a hot summer's day."

– Mary Kennedy,
Author of The Dream Club Mysteries

"I'm a huge fan of Kathi's books. I think I've read every one. Without a doubt, she's a gifted cozy mystery author and I eagerly await each new release!"

– Dianne Harman,
Author of the High Desert Cozy Mysteries

"Intriguing, likeable characters, keep-you-guessing mysteries, and settings that literally transport you to Paradise...Daley's stories draw you in and keep you glued until the very last page."

– Tracy Weber,
Agatha-Nominated Author of the Downward Dog Mysteries

"Daley really knows how to write a top-notch cozy."

– *MJB Reviewers*

"Kathi Daley writes a story with a puzzling cold-case mystery while highlighting...the love of home, family, and good friends."

– *Chatting About Cozies*

Bikinis
IN
PARADISE

The Tj Jensen Mystery Series
by Kathi Daley

Bikinis
IN
PARADISE

A
TJ JENSEN
MYSTERY

KATHI DALEY

HENERY PRESS

BIKINIS IN PARADISE
A Tj Jensen Mystery
Part of the Henery Press Mystery Collection

Second Edition | September 2016

Henery Press, LLC
www.henerypress.com

Trade Paperback ISBN-13: 978-1-63511-097-5
Digital epub ISBN-13: 978-1-63511-098-2
Kindle ISBN-13: 978-1-63511-099-9
Hardcover Paperback ISBN-13: 978-1-63511-100-2

Printed in the United States of America

This book is dedicated to my sister Christy Turner
who is also my very best friend.

ACKNOWLEDGMENTS

They say it takes a village and I have a great one.

I want to thank all my friends who hang out over at my Kathi Daley Books Group page on Facebook. This exceptional group help me not only with promotion but with helpful suggestion and feedback as well.

I want to thank the bloggers who have pretty much adopted me and have helped me to build a fantastic social media presence. There are too many to list but I want to specifically recognize Amy Brantley for taking in a brand new author and showing me the ropes.

I want to thank my fellow authors who I run to all the time when I don't know how to do something or how to deal with a situation. I have to say that the cozy mystery family is about as close-knit a family as you are likely to find anywhere.

I want to thank Bruce Curran for generously helping me with all my techy questions and Ricky Turner for help with my webpage.

I want to thank my graphic designer Jessica Fisher for all my flashy ads and headers.

I want to thank Randy Ladenheim-Gil for making what I write legible.

I want to thank Art Molinares for welcoming me so enthusiastically to the Henery Press family and a special thank you to Erin George and the entire editing crew who have been so incredibly awesome and fun to work with.

And last but certainly not least, I want to thank my super-husband Ken for allowing me time to write by taking care of everything else (and I mean everything).

CHAPTER 1

Wednesday, June 18

"In all your life, have you ever seen so many butts?" Amber Walton, Maggie's Hideaway's newest employee, commented as twenty-five scantily-dressed models gathered on the lawn in front of the lodge. The Tropical Tan Corporation, which had been selling tanning lotion for the past fifty years, took selecting Ms. Tropical Tan seriously. Not only was each contestant physically fit and genetically blessed, but each model was tasked with proving her overall intelligence as well as her ability to speak articulately in front of a crowd of people.

"It does seem like the suits get smaller every year," Tj Jensen agreed. She watched as the fans lined up to talk to their favorite model. Each and every finalist for the spokesmodel contest was darkly tanned and exceptionally beautiful. The judges were going to have a difficult time picking one winner out of the group.

"When the girl with the skin-colored thong showed up, I had to take a second look to make sure she had on anything at all," Amber said. "I know it's not polite to stare, and I tried to look away, but my eyes keep driftin' back."

Tj laughed. "They don't have bikinis where you come from?"

"Not like the ones these girls are wearin'."

"The models are all eager to make a good first impression," Tj explained as the models greeted the group of men and women who had gathered to meet them. "Popularity is an important factor to the judges when deciding who will make the best spokesmodel, so the girl with the biggest following from the crowd usually wins."

"If my mama was here, she'd be runnin' around prayin' for these girls' salvation while wrappin' every one of them in one of the towels housekeepin' has stacked by the pool."

Tj laughed. "I need to get everyone registered. Will you be okay?"

"Yes, Miss Tj. Just point me in the right direction."

"Just Tj," she reminded the girl.

"Sorry, ma'am. I'll try to remember."

"Why don't you go help get the bar set up for the orientation?" Tj suggested. "Logan knows what needs to be done, so just do whatever he asks."

"Yes, Miss Tj. I'll do that right away."

Amber was a nice enough girl and a hard worker, but she'd been so isolated from everyday life that she was awkward and unsure in everyday situations. Hiring her had been activity director Julie Sorenson's idea, and Tj trusted Julie's instincts. Tj had been skeptical at first, but after a few weeks on the job, she had to admit Amber was a bright girl with a curious mind who could very well do great things if given the chance.

"Can I have everyone's attention?" Tj yelled into the megaphone she was holding as Amber scurried away. All twenty-five models had prospered in the months of regional competitions leading up to this point, and every one of the girls, aged eighteen to twenty-four, was determined to win the title as well as the twenty-five thousand dollars in prize money. To say there was an element of competition in the air was putting it mildly.

"I'd like to welcome you all to the final weekend of the Ms. Tropical Tan spokesmodel competition. The staff from Tropical Tan Deep Tanning Lotion has planned a fast-paced few days. The winner will be crowned during the farewell festivities on Sunday afternoon."

Tj waited for the drone of conversation to die down. Who knew being a spokesmodel for a popular brand of tanning lotion could be such a competitive process? Every one of the twenty-five beautiful women left in the mix could easily sell tankers of the popular tan enhancer to the multitudes of men who followed the contest from town to town. The Tropical Tan folks had booked the entire resort for the long weekend, but Tj knew the lodging properties in Serenity, to the north of the resort, and Indulgence, to the south, were booked with spectators waiting to root for their favorite contestant.

"If I could direct your attention to the tables behind me, we have room assignments and calendars for everyone," Tj continued. "The first station is being manned by our lodging manager, Leiani Pope." Leiani, a native Hawaiian, looked like she could be a competitor herself, with her bronze skin, flawless complexion, and long black hair. "Leiani will provide you with your room assignment and meal card."

"After you receive your room assignment, you can make your way over to the table to your left, where our activities director, Julie Sorenson, will give you your schedule for the weekend." Julie was as blond and bubbly as Leiani was dark and serious. "As most of you know, the Tropical Tan committee will be on-site tomorrow to begin judging the various competitions.

Today is unscheduled, so feel free to enjoy our white sand beach, heated pool, the Lakeside Bar and Grill, or any of the other amenities we provide."

"Is the pool area clothing optional?" An anorexic-looking woman with long legs, black hair, and a deep tan asked.

"No. This is a family resort and we require that proper swim attire be worn at all times," Tj answered.

"I thought Tropical Tan booked the entire resort for the weekend," the woman argued.

"They have, but the sand that borders Maggie's Hideaway is a public beach, and the pool area is clearly visible from the beach."

"Do you have a spa?" An even taller woman with dark skin, long blond hair, and 2 percent body fat asked. "I'm going to need a daily facial in this dry climate."

"The Tropical Tan people have arranged for their personnel to be on-site," Tj said.

Tj wasn't one to obsess about her looks, but every year when this particular group of guests showed up, she couldn't help but compare her petite frame, frizzy auburn hair, and freckled nose with these women, who made a career out of looking perfect in every situation. Not that Tj would want to go to all the effort they put into their appearance. She had been raised in an all-male household and was considered by most to be a tomboy.

"Are there any other questions?" Tj asked.

Luckily, no one replied. Tj set down the megaphone as the women lined up and began checking in. "I thought someone from Tropical Tan was supposed to be here to help with the orientation," Tj said to Leiani, who had turned her station over to one of the desk clerks.

"A woman by the name of Tonya Overton was supposed to

accompany the models from the airport. I don't know what happened to her," Leiani replied.

Tj remembered Tonya from the planning meeting she and her father had attended with the Tropical Tan staff a couple of months earlier. She knew the woman had been in the area a couple of weeks ago as well. "Maybe her flight was delayed," Tj said. "Why don't you call the Tropical Tan folks and see if they've heard from her?"

"Okay. I'll head inside and make the call," Leiani said.

Tj looked out toward the lake as she waited. It was a beautiful early summer day. The snow in the alpine basin had melted completely, leaving miles of white sand beach as a buffer between the evergreen forest and the crystal-clear but cold mountain lake.

Tj loved this time of year. The brightly colored umbrellas the resort stored each winter had been set up on the deck of the Lakeside Bar and Grill, providing diners with a beachfront view as they enjoyed the variety of offerings their chef cooked up each day. While Tropical Tan Week was a moneymaker for the resort, Tj preferred the atmosphere when the campground was filled with families who came to the area each summer to swim in the water and hike the isolated trails winding through the desolate forest. Many of the regulars who returned year after year felt more like family than customers.

"We only had twenty-four models check in," the desk clerk who had taken over for Leiani informed Tj after the last model had made it through the first line.

"Twenty-four? Who's missing?"

"Kiara Boswell."

Tj picked up the megaphone she'd been using. "Has anyone seen Kiara Boswell?" she yelled.

"She was on the bus," the tall blonde who'd asked about the

spa answered. "There was a man waiting for her when we pulled up. They headed toward the beach."

Tj frowned. The models knew they were to show up for registration. The last thing Tj needed this week was to babysit a model wannabe who was more interested in boys than bikinis. While Tj didn't consider herself to be an old woman at twenty-eight, the average age of the Tropical Tan contestant was nineteen. This was the third year that the resort had hosted the event, and every year there'd been at least one model who had caused Tj a significant amount of angst. To make matters worse, this year Tj's father was out of town, leaving her in charge of the resort.

"I'll go look for her," Tj offered. "Do we have a photo of our missing model?"

"I think Leiani has one," the desk clerk said.

Tj went into the lodge, where Leiani was still on the phone. She checked her messages while she waited for her lodging manager to complete her conversation. The lodge had undergone a facelift over the winter, and the wall of windows that looked out over the lake was now framed with log poles that looked like tree trunks. Tj felt they gave the illusion that the forest continued inside the structure. Several overstuffed sofas were arranged around the floor-to-ceiling river-rock fireplace that served as the focal point for the mountain-themed room. The reception area was open to the second floor, where artfully decorated rooms were provided for those preferring a less expensive alternative to the cabins that were normally booked from June through October.

Tj snagged a freshly baked cookie from the sideboard, where coffee, tea, and pastries were kept ready for their guests during the day. Most times the cookie offerings needed to be replenished every few hours, but Tj bet that dust would gather on the double chocolate chews the chef had provided while the models were in residence as their only guests.

"Okay, thanks," Tj heard Leiani say before she hung up.

"Tonya was on the flight from Miami but didn't show up at the bus," Leiani informed Tj. "The Tropical Tan people are going to look into it. They asked that we just handle the orientation the best we can. They assured me they'd send Tonya up the hill as soon as they located her and promised the rest of the crew would be here tomorrow, as planned."

"It seems we have another problem," Tj said. "One of the models didn't check in."

"Who?"

"Kiara Boswell. The other girls said a tall man with blond hair met her at the bus, and she left with him when she disembarked. I'm going to go to look for her. Do we have a photo?"

"Yeah." Leiani sorted through a stack of files on the desk. After a short search, she pulled out the right one. She opened the cover and handed Tj a headshot.

The girl was beautiful. Long brown hair, a petite form, huge blue eyes, and a welcoming smile that greeted you like a warm embrace. "She looks familiar," Tj commented as she studied the photo. "Has she visited with us before?"

"According to the file, she listed Serenity, Nevada, as her hometown."

"Really? It's odd I don't know her." Tj took the file from Leiani. "It says here she's eighteen. She must not have attended Serenity High School or I'd have had her in one of my classes at some point." Tj was a teacher and coach at the local high school.

"Maybe she was homeschooled," Leiani suggested.

"Yeah, maybe. Go ahead and get everyone else settled. I'll see if I can find our missing model."

CHAPTER 2

Tj returned to the lawn and called her dog, Echo, who had been napping in the shade, to her side as she headed to the beach. It had been such a busy day that she hadn't been able to take Echo for a run that morning. It made sense to kill two birds with one stone, getting Echo the exercise he needed while she looked for the missing girl. The weather in June in the Paradise Mountains could be unpredictable. While most years they had beautiful weather, it wasn't unheard of to get a late snowstorm as well. Thankfully, Mother Nature had been generous this year, and the daytime temperatures hovered in the mid-seventies, while the nighttime temperatures dropped into the forties.

Tj was trying to decide whether to walk to the north or the south when she was greeted by a young girl of about twelve or thirteen. The girl had long and thick, if somewhat stringy, blond hair. She had the most amazing blue eyes and a wide smile, which provided a welcoming appearance in spite of the fact that she wore a tattered yellow dress and worn tennis shoes with no socks.

"Can I help you with something?" Tj asked.

"Are you the lady who's looking for Kiara?" the girl asked.

"How did you know I was looking for Kiara?"

"One of the ladies over where the girls are signing in told

me that Kiara hadn't checked in, but one of the staff was looking for her."

"Do you know Kiara?"

"I'm her sister. Half-sister, really. Kiara and I share a father." Tj immediately recognized the resemblance to the photo of the model. "Kiara was supposed to be here, but I can't find her." The poor girl looked like she might cry.

"What's your name?" Tj asked.

"Annabeth."

"My name is Tj. I suspected you might be Kiara's sister. You're very beautiful. Just like she is."

Annabeth grinned. "You think so?"

"I do."

"So you've seen my sister?"

"Actually, no," Tj admitted. "I saw a photo of her, though. Kiara was on the bus, but she left shortly after she arrived with a tall man with blond hair. Do you know who that might be?"

The girl looked around. "I have to go," she said before running back toward the resort.

"Odd," Tj muttered. She was worried about the girl but really needed to find the model. She called Leiani on her cell and asked her to keep an eye out for Annabeth, and then headed down the beach to the north.

Tj waved to several people she knew as she trudged through the hot sand. She loved the community she lived in. Like most of her peers, she'd gone away to college, but unlike many who chose to relocate to larger towns with more opportunities, Tj had come home the minute she graduated. She was lucky to get a job as a teacher at the local high school. As with most of the staff in the small high school, she took on many duties, including coaching the track team in the spring, the girls' soccer team in the fall, and the ski team in the winter.

Tj took off her flip-flops and walked barefoot through the warm sand. Although it was a weekday afternoon in mid-June, it seemed everyone had decided to take advantage of the gorgeous weather. Families shared picnic lunches, while younger kids played in the sand and older ones played in the water. Tj didn't know how she was going to find one girl among the crowd. She waved to a group of high school students she recognized before heading in their direction. Maybe one or more of them had seen the girl walk by. She really was a beautiful young woman. Even if the girls hadn't noticed her, Tj was certain the boys would have.

"Hey, Coach," Connor Harrington, one of her favorite students, called out. "Out for a walk?"

"Actually, I'm looking for this girl." Tj handed the boy the photo. "She's one of the models staying at the resort for the bikini competition, but she never checked in."

"Yeah, I saw her. She walked by about a half hour ago."

"Was she with anyone?"

"A tall guy with short blond hair."

"Did you see which way she went?" Tj asked.

"She was walking down the beach toward the cove."

Secret Cove was isolated, normally accessed by boat since it could only be reached by land by climbing down a fairly steep embankment.

"If the model comes back by, will you remind her that she's needed at the resort?" Tj asked.

"Sure thing."

Tj wondered if she should get back to the resort and just let the missing model find her own way back. She would certainly be penalized for not adhering to protocol by checking in and attending the orientation with the other models, but Kiara was an adult and therefore responsible for her own bad choices. On the other hand, walking along the lakeshore was a much more desirable activity than overseeing the orientation, which Leiani and Julie could handle just fine without her. After a bit of consideration, Tj continued on to the cove. If Kiara wasn't there, chances were she'd run into her as she returned to the resort.

The sandy beach became less densely populated with sunbathers as she left the area where the resort was located and continued on toward the north. The only way to get to the cove was via a rocky trail that left the beach and wound through the forest for a time before returning to the lakeshore. By the time Tj ran out of beach, it was already more than forty minutes since she'd left Maggie's Hideaway. She was debating whether to continue when she remembered the panicked look on the face of the girl's sister. Annabeth seemed afraid of the man who met Kiara. Perhaps the model was in danger and needed to be rescued.

Tj stood at the top of the trail where it looped back down toward the beach. The small strip of white sand that bordered Secret Cove was deserted. Tj felt her phone vibrate when she was halfway down the path. She paused to answer.

"Did you find her?" Leiani asked.

"No. I'm at the cove now, but I don't see her. I'm going to head back," Tj replied.

"I spoke to one of the other models. She didn't think Kiara left willingly with the man who was waiting for her," Leiani informed her. "She said Kiara seemed surprised to see him when she got off the bus. According to the girl who was sitting just behind her, the man grabbed her arm and pulled her to the side. It appeared they were arguing, but after a minute or two, Kiara followed him toward the beach."

"Did you manage to track down the sister?"

"No. I looked around, but there was no sign of her."

"Okay. I'll see you in a few minutes."

Tj turned to head back toward the resort when Echo took off down the path.

"Echo," Tj called, but her normally obedient dog ignored her. "Echo," she tried again, before following down the steep trail.

The dog ran to the edge of the waterline and looked out toward the horizon.

"Echo, there's nothing out there. Now let's go; it's getting late."

The dog barked and swam into the water. Tj got a chill down her spine. There was only one reason Echo would flat-out disobey an order.

"Damn."

CHAPTER 3

Tj hugged her sometimes boyfriend and lead deputy for the Serenity branch of the Paradise Lake Sheriff's Department, Dylan Caine. He'd arrived with fellow deputy Roy Fisher shortly after she'd called 911. Based on the direction from which they'd arrived, Tj assumed they'd parked on the road and then hiked down the steep embankment.

"She's about thirty yards out in approximately twenty feet of water," Tj told Dylan as she fought to control her shivering. The lake water was freezing at this time of year, and the cove was entirely in the shade at this time of day. "It looks like she's been hit on the head. I would have tried to bring her in, but she's been weighted."

Dylan took off his shirt and wrapped it around Tj. In any other situation, she would have stopped to notice how gorgeous Dylan looked in the tank top he wore under his shirt, but the only thing Tj could see now were the empty eyes of the woman as she stared at her after she'd dove down to the spot Echo had led her to. Luckily, Tj was a triathlete and an excellent swimmer. The lake claimed more than one victim a year who underestimated the deadly combination of cold water and sheer drop-offs.

"And you said you recognize the woman?" Dylan asked.

"Yes. Her name is Tonya Overton. She works for the Tropical Tan Corporation. She was new this year, but Dad and I met her during the planning meeting we had with the administration a few months ago. And she made another trip here to verify photoshoot locations a couple weeks ago. She was supposed to accompany the girls to the resort, but she never made it to the bus. Leiani spoke to someone from the Florida office who confirmed she flew into Reno from Miami today."

"So how did she get here if she didn't come on the bus?" Dylan stated the obvious.

"I have no idea."

"And you said you were looking for a missing model when you found the body?"

"Yes. One of the girls was met at the bus by a man the other girls described as being tall with blond hair. They headed toward the beach together. I ran into one of my students on the beach, and he said he saw her walking toward the cove with a man fitting the same description."

"Could the missing model have been meeting Ms. Overton?" Dylan asked.

Tj hadn't considered it, but the idea that the two missing women were connected in some way made sense. "I really don't know. I do know that based on the information provided in the missing model's file, Kiara Boswell listed Serenity as her hometown. As far as I can remember, she didn't go through our school system, but she could have been homeschooled. I believe Tonya is from Miami originally, but she's been to Serenity on two occasions, so it seems reasonable she could have met people who live in the area."

"Right now you need to get out of those wet clothes. We're going to be here a while. I've called for the divers, but it could be more than an hour until they arrive. I'll have Roy drive you and

Echo back to the resort. I'll come by when I'm done here."

"Honestly, it's almost as far up to the road as it is back to the resort along the beach. I'll just walk so Roy can stay to help you," Tj offered.

Dylan held her by the shoulders and looked deeply into her eyes. "Are you sure you're okay? Finding the girl under the water like that must have been quite a shock."

"I'm fine," Tj assured him. "This isn't my first body, you know."

Dylan frowned. "Yeah, I guess not. Call me when you get back to the resort so I know you're okay."

"Yes, Dad." Tj stood on tiptoe to kiss Dylan, who was more than a foot taller than her, on the lips. She grinned as Dylan blushed. Kissing the officer who responded to a murder call probably wasn't proper etiquette, but Tj had endured a long day, and a quick kiss from the man she was growing to care for was just what she needed to get her through the rest of it.

Tj took off his shirt and handed it back to Dylan. "You should probably be dressed when the others arrive. The sun will be hitting the beach once I get around the bend, so I'll be fine."

"Are you sure?" Dylan accepted the partially wet shirt.

"I'm sure. I'll see you later."

Tj called Echo to her side and started back up the rocky path. She wanted to be good and gone before the divers arrived and brought Tonya to the surface. Tj had seen dead bodies before, but there was something particularly disturbing about seeing the young woman floating in the water with her eyes open and her long hair floating around her like a halo. Whoever killed her had tied one of her legs to an anchor before dumping her.

Tj had called and spoken to Leiani while she waited for Dylan to arrive. Leiani agreed to go ahead with the orientation without mentioning the dead woman in the cove. She never had been able to track down the young girl Tj had spoken to on the beach. Tj couldn't help but wonder where she had gone off to, and how she had come to be there. She was too young to make the trip from town to the resort on her own, so she must have arrived with someone. Someone, Tj supposed, who might be looking for Kiara as well.

By the time she made it back around to the beach, Connor and the other students were gone. Tj decided that was a good thing. She didn't feel up to casual conversation, and she suspected Dylan wouldn't want her talking about the murder until he had a chance to notify the next of kin. The sun hitting her shoulders felt wonderful. She'd dressed for the day in khaki shorts, a yellow tank top, and a hooded Maggie's Hideaway sweatshirt. She'd discarded the sweatshirt before she'd left to find Kiara, but now she was wishing she'd had the foresight to bring it along when she left the resort.

Although Maggie's Hideaway was the largest resort on Paradise Lake, it wasn't that far of a walk back to the private house where Tj lived with her dad, grandpa, and half-sisters.

"What happened to you?" Grandpa Ben asked when she walked in through the front door. Ben was tall and broad-shouldered, a mountain of a man with white hair, bright blue eyes, and a deep baritone voice that demanded to be heard.

"You didn't hear?"

"I just got back from town and haven't talked to anyone. Is something wrong?"

"One of the Tropical Tan girls didn't check in. I went to look for her."

"Did you find her?"

"No, but I found Tonya Overton. She's dead."

"Dead?" Ben asked. "What happened?"

"It looks like someone hit her over the head and then dumped her in the lake. Give me a few minutes to clean the sand off Echo and shower, and I'll fill you in."

"I'll take care of Echo," Ben offered. "And I'll make a pot of coffee. Go ahead and get cleaned up, and then you can tell me what happened."

"Okay, Grandpa. Thanks. Did the girls call?"

"Yeah. Everyone is safe and sound in Florida. They were sorry you couldn't make the trip but very excited to be going to Disney World."

"I'm going to miss them," Tj realized. "I'll have to call them tomorrow."

Tj walked up the stairs to her room. Her dad had been signed up to be part of a panel discussion on tourism at a conference in Florida. When Ashley, who had just turned nine, and Gracie, who was almost six, heard he was going to be staying in Orlando, they'd begged and pleaded until her dad agreed to take them with him so they could finally go to Disney World. Her dad's girlfriend, Rosalie, had offered to go on the trip to keep an eye on the girls while her dad was tied up. Tj appreciated how fully her dad and grandpa had accepted the girls into their lives, even though neither were actually related to them by blood. Ashley and Gracie were the products of her mother's second marriage to a man named Walton Reynolds, who, as far as she knew, hadn't contacted his daughters a single time since he'd left home when Gracie was only two months old.

With Mike away, Tj and Ben were left with the task of babysitting the Tropical Tan girls. Tj had to admit she didn't entirely understand the competitive frenzy the girls worked themselves into during the final weekend of the competition. The idea of prancing around in front of a huge crowd mainly comprised of male members of the community who whistled and called out suggestions inappropriate for all but the raunchiest of conversations didn't appeal to her in the least.

Tj dropped her damp clothes in the hamper before turning on the water in the large tile shower. Standing under the powerful spray, she willed herself to relax. She should call the Tropical Tan people and let them know the woman they'd hired to accompany the girls was dead. Chances were, the sheriff's office would want to inform the other contestants about the situation as well. Although she'd only met Tonya a couple of times, the woman seemed nice, and Tj couldn't help but wonder who had killed her, and why.

After she showered and liberally applied a scented lotion to her body, she dressed in jeans, a t-shirt, and a zip-up sweatshirt. She finger-styled her long, curly hair and slipped a pair of worn Nike's on her feet. By the time she made her way downstairs, Echo was happily napping and Ben was sitting at the kitchen counter with a cup of coffee in front of him.

"Dylan called," Ben announced.

"I was supposed to call him," Tj admitted.

"He figured you forgot. When you didn't answer your cell, he called the house phone."

"Did they get the body up?"

"Yeah. Dylan is pretty sure the victim was hit with a rock or some other hard object and then sank, as you suspected. Coffee?" Ben held up the coffeepot.

"Sure."

"Do you think Tonya's murder and the missing model are connected?" Ben asked.

"I have no idea. I suppose we should try to find out who Kiara left with. And if she isn't back, we should try to get a more detailed description from the other girls."

"Why don't you call Leiani to see if Kiara is back? If she

isn't, I'll call Doc to see if he's free to come over." Doc was one of Ben's best friends, retired coroner Stan Griffin. "He has a real gift with a pencil. I'm betting he can draw what the eyewitnesses describe. Maybe we can track down the man from the sketch. If we can find the man she left with, maybe we can find the model."

"Okay. Let me call Dylan first to make sure it's okay for us to talk to the girls. He may want us to wait until someone from the sheriff's office can come by."

By the time Tj got through to Dylan, he was going over the site with a fine-tooth comb to see what, if any, physical evidence he could turn up. He preferred Tj didn't fill the girls in on Tonya's death, but was okay with her continuing her search for Kiara, who Leiani verified still hadn't shown up. Tj looked at the clock. The models should still be in orientation. Leiani already knew what was going on, so Tj decided to call her to request that she keep the girls occupied in the bar until Doc arrived. That way they wouldn't have to round everyone up again.

Twenty minutes later, Tj watched as a shiny red '57 Chevrolet with white vinyl seats and chrome wheels parked in the private drive next to the house. A man of average build with a few extra pounds around the middle, dressed in a red-and-white Hawaiian print shirt and perfectly pressed khakis, waved as he opened the driver's door and climbed out. If there was one word that would best describe Doc, it was loud. He wore bright colors, spoke with a booming voice, enjoyed off-color jokes, and had a reputation as being the biggest flirt the Serenity Senior Center had seen for quite some time.

"I hear you managed to find yourself another body." Doc wrapped his arms around her in a hug.

"Not intentionally. One of the bikini girls went missing, and in the process of looking for her, I found our missing Tropical Tan rep. Thanks for coming on such short notice."

"No problem. You know I'm always happy to lend a hand during the bikini competition."

Tj smiled. "I guess I should have known you'd find a way to enjoy helping me with a missing persons investigation. Dylan is fine with us continuing the search for Kiara but doesn't want us mentioning Tonya's death to anyone just yet. Our main objective this afternoon is to find out what we can about Kiara, and get a description of the man who met her at the bus."

"Does Dylan think the missing girl is connected to the death in some way?" Doc asked.

"He isn't ruling out the possibility."

Doc and Tj headed over to the Lakeside Bar and Grill, where the girls were just completing their orientation. Tj made a general announcement to the girls that Kiara was still missing, and that they needed to interview the girls about the incident at the bus. Tj sat at one of the dining tables in the bar with Doc beside her, and Leiani organized the interviews. Maggie's Hideaway's bar manager, Logan Cole, mixed drinks for the models while Leiani sent them to be interviewed one at a time.

The first model sent to speak to them was last year's runner-up. She was tall and thin, with blond hair and green eyes. Like all of the models in the competition, she had a tan that must have taken hours in a tanning booth to perfect. Now that the spectators who had met the bus had moved on to other things, most of the models had changed into shorts or skirts and casual tops. Jazzy, on the other hand, had chosen to dress in the tiniest bikini Tj had ever seen, with only a very transparent wrap as a concession to the Bar and Grill's shirt-and-shoes policy.

"I need you to tell me everything you saw after the bus

arrived," Tj told the woman with caked silver glitter on her eyelids.

"I was sitting behind Kiara on the bus. When we arrived at the resort, I was behind her as we disembarked. There was a man waiting for her."

"And what did this man look like?" Tj asked.

"He was tall. He had broad shoulders and short blond hair. One of those razor cuts people get in the military. He had on a loose-fitting shirt, but based on his arms, I'm willing to bet he sported a pretty fine six pack. I didn't notice his eye color. He was dressed in jeans and a blue t-shirt and had on heavy boots. The kind with a hard toe and a rubber heel. I remember thinking that he was way overdressed for the warm weather. I mean, why go to all that trouble to develop guns if you're going to cover up even in the summer?"

"Can you describe the shape of the man's face?" Doc asked.

The girl looked confused. "His face?"

"Oval, round, square?" Doc clarified.

"I don't know." The woman shrugged. "To be honest, I really wasn't looking at his face."

"I know this is difficult for you, but I need you to try to remember what you saw," Tj encouraged. "Kiara could very well be in some type of trouble. It's important that we find her as soon as possible."

"Okay." Jazzy looked intently at the drawing Doc was working on. "He had a rounder face, fuller cheeks, and a dimple in his chin."

"Like this?" Doc made a few adjustments and then held up the sketch.

"Yeah, only his eyes were different. I didn't see the color, but they were small and closer together."

Doc made the adjustments. "Better?"

Jazzy bit her lip as she studied the drawing. "His eyebrows were bushier, and he had the longest eyelashes."

"Any other facial hair?" Doc asked.

"No, he was clean-cut. He had a scar at the corner of one eye." The woman scrunched up her face as she thought about it. "Brown; I think his eyes were brown. Or maybe dark blue. They were dark."

It seemed that the model had noticed quite a lot about the man she claimed to have only gotten a glimpse of.

"Okay, how is this?" Doc held up the sketch again.

"That's pretty darn close," the girl said.

"After Kiara got off the bus, you saw the man grab her by the arm and pull her to the side?" Tj asked.

"Yeah, he pulled her far enough away so that I couldn't hear what they were saying, but it was obvious they were arguing."

"Did Kiara seem scared when she first noticed the man?"

"No." Jazzy thought about it. "Not scared but mad."

"And after they argued?"

"They headed toward the beach."

"Was Kiara struggling?" Tj asked.

"No, it looked like she went with him willingly. He wasn't holding onto her and he didn't appear to have a weapon or anything. There were tons of people around, so I imagine if she didn't want to leave with him, she could have called out or something."

"Can you remember anything else?" Tj asked.

"No. Sorry. I wasn't paying that much attention. To be honest, I was more focused on the spectators who had arrived to meet the bus. There's this one guy who has been following the tour for the past month. All the girls have a thing for him, but I'm pretty sure I'm the one he comes to see."

Tj didn't understand why anyone would take time out of

their life to follow a bunch of women around the country, but apparently it occurred more often than one would think.

"Are we about done here?" Jazzy began to tap her long acrylic nails on the table in a show of impatience. Tj understood the models had better things to do than answer their questions, but one girl was missing and another woman was dead. Of course, Jazzy and the others didn't know that Tonya was dead. As far as they knew, Kiara had simply taken off with a cute guy who met her at the bus.

"I realize we're asking a lot of questions and that Kiara may very well be off on a date, but all of the models are our responsibility, and as such, it's up to us to make sure everyone is safe and accounted for. I hope you understand."

"I've told you everything I know." Jazzy looked toward the other room, where the girls were drinking and seemingly having a good time.

"I know you'd like to get back to what you were doing, but we have a few more questions, if you can bear with us." Tj pasted on her friendliest smile.

"Okay." Jazzy sighed. "What do you want to know?"

"Did Kiara mention a name when she first noticed the man who met the bus?" Tj asked.

"A name?"

"Yeah, did she say something like 'Bill, what are you doing here?'"

"No. Not that I can remember."

"Did she say anything at all?"

"She did ask the man what he was doing there, but I don't remember her saying his name."

"And how did the man respond?"

"He said something like 'we have to talk,' and then he pulled her aside. I didn't hear anything after that."

"How long have you known Kiara?" Tj asked.

Jazzy shrugged. "I don't know. I guess about a month. This weekend is the final competition for the spokesmodel gig, but there were a series of regional competitions leading up to this point. I'm from San Francisco and Kiara is representing Los Angeles, so we're both part of the western division, although initially I was grouped with the north, while she was grouped with the south."

"North and south?"

"In the beginning, there were more than a hundred girls in our division, so the field was divided into the northern section and the southern section. Once the groups were whittled down a bit, the north and south were combined, and that's when I met Kiara. Farah, who represents San Diego, has probably known her the longest; they would have been competing in the same group from the start."

Tj made a note to speak to Farah next.

"Did she ever mention having a sister?" Tj asked. The girl on the beach seemed to know the man who met Kiara. If they could find her, it would make things a lot easier.

"No, she never mentioned having any family, but we really didn't talk about our lives outside of the competition."

"Had she said anything to you about being frightened or feeling threatened by anyone in the time you've known her?"

"No. Honestly, I barely spoke to her. She was pretty shy and didn't socialize much with the other girls. The only reason she even entered the competition was for the scholarship."

"Scholarship?"

"The winner of the competition not only gets a jumpstart on her modeling career, but there's a cash prize as well as a significant scholarship to the college of your choice. Personally, I'm more interested in what winning this competition can do for my modeling career, but Kiara was in it for the scholarship."

"We plan to speak to all of the models, but is there anyone Kiara was particularly close to? Anyone she might have been more apt to confide in than the others?" Tj asked.

"Chloe is the quietest and most serious of the group. She was sitting next to Kiara on the bus, on the aisle. She got off just in front of her. I guess she might have something to add."

"Okay, thank you. Please let me know if you think of anything else."

Tj interviewed each girl in turn. Many had been in front of Kiara on the bus, so they'd already been at the check-in area before the altercation occurred and hadn't seen anything. Of those who witnessed the exchange, there seemed to be a pretty big discrepancy as to exactly how tall the man was and whether or not he had light eyes or dark. Everyone agreed on the basic look of the man, as well as the length and color of his hair.

Farah had known Kiara the longest, but she reported that they weren't really friends. Farah was aggressively pursuing an acting career and was interested in the competition only to the extent it could help her in her mission to land a major role before her twenty-first birthday. Chloe was representing the Midwest and had just recently joined the tour but was able to confirm Kiara was very much focused on getting the scholarship. No one they spoke to knew if Kiara had a sister or any other family.

"So what do you think?" Tj asked Doc after they'd interviewed all the girls.

"I think based on what the girls have said, this Kiara doesn't seem like a typical bikini model. Maybe the man who met her was an old friend who convinced her to drop out of the contest."

"Yeah, maybe. I'd feel better if we could track her down and verify that. I might not be as concerned, but I have an uneasy feeling about things after what happened to Tonya. The high school kids I ran into on the beach confirmed Kiara was heading toward the same cove where I found Tonya's body."

"Let's make a few copies of my drawing and start asking around. Someone must have seen her."

CHAPTER 4

After Doc left, Tj helped Leiani and Julie with the remaining twenty-four beauty contestants. By the time the sun had completed its descent behind the mountain, the bar was rocking with bikini models strutting their stuff to the music provided by the vintage jukebox her dad had found in an antique store. Luckily, Logan was an easygoing sort of guy who rolled with the punches as stress relief turned to drunken acts of outrageousness. Between the girls gone wild in the bar, the dead body in the cove, and not knowing what had happened to Kiara, Tj was about to jump out of her skin. It seemed like Logan and Julie had things handled in the bar, so Tj decided to go for a walk to try to unwind and gear up for the long weekend.

Maggie's Hideaway made out well by giving over the entire facility to the Tropical Tan people every year; they paid a substantial amount of money for the exclusive use of the resort, and the national attention the competition generated brought free advertising and exposure to the area. Julie Sorenson had been instrumental in turning the competition into a four-day event. While the various spokesmodel contests were the highlights, the resort offered activities that appealed to a wide range of spectators, including a water-ski show, a stand-up paddleboard race, a sunset boat parade, an arts and crafts fair, a barbecue cook-off, and a home brewer's competition. When the weather cooperated, as it had this year, the beaches around the lake were packed with sunbathers anxious to get started on their summer fun.

The largest single draw, other than the models, was probably the fireworks over the lake on Sunday night. The larger casinos in Indulgence got together to put on the fabulous display, which was choreographed to music that could be experienced by tuning into Indulgence's one and only radio station. Tj suspected the casino owners had decided to have the event on Sunday rather than Saturday night to encourage out-of-town guests to stay an extra night.

Tj stopped to embrace the quiet of the evening. Most of the beachgoers had gone home, leaving only a few stargazers on the mostly deserted beach. If you closed your eyes, you could feel the warm night air embrace you as the waves churned up by the boats lapped gently onto the shore. Tj had lived at Maggie's Hideaway almost her entire life, and at times she got so busy that she forgot to stop and enjoy the scenery. But no matter how busy she was, she knew she would never take a perfect summer evening for granted.

After confirming that the models were set for the evening, Tj returned to an empty house. Ben had offered to cancel his plans with his friends, but she had convinced him she'd enjoy some quiet time to herself. She had to admit, however, that she was beginning to regret the decision. After everything that had happened, she wished there were people around to distract her from her thoughts.

She wiped the sand from her feet and Echo's paws, then poured herself a glass of wine and turned on the stereo. It was a soft-jazz sort of night. Something relaxing to calm her nerves, while the models were rocking it out in the bar with the spectators who had chosen to stick around. Although it had been a warm day, it was chilly in the evening, so Tj lit the fire someone had already built in the fireplace.

Once she settled in, the four household cats joined her on the sofa. Echo, who was really too big for the sofa, was curled up at Tj's feet. She sipped her wine and let the harmony of purring cats calm her soul. As the music changed from jazz to soothing piano, Tj thought about the long day she'd had. Her dad, Rosalie, and the girls had left for the airport at four a.m., and Tj had gotten up to see them off. She'd intended to go back to bed, but she was wide awake by the time they pulled away, so she'd made a pot of coffee and used the time to plan her day.

With her dad away, the bulk of the responsibility for managing the resort fell to her. Her grandpa helped out, but he had long since retired, so Tj tried to pick up the bulk of the slack. She'd met with all the managers to ensure that everything was in place for the Tropical Tan people. On one hand, the fact that they'd booked the entire resort made life just a bit easier. During the summer, when the campground was open, there were as many as a hundred and fifty guests at any one time. In comparison, twenty-five models plus ten staff from Tropical Tan made for an easy weekend. Or so it would seem. So far, things hadn't started off easy at all.

Tj was debating whether or not to pour herself a second glass of wine when the cell phone on the table beside her began to ring.

"Dylan," Tj responded to the caller ID. "Any news?"

"The coroner puts the cause of death as blunt force trauma to the head, and it looks like the weapon was a rock," Dylan answered. "The time of death was within sixty minutes of when you arrived. Did you notice anyone in the area?"

"No, no one," Tj said as she tucked her feet up under her legs and snuggled Cuervo to her chest. "When I arrived at the top of the trail that overlooks the cove, I looked around. I was trying to decide if it was worth it to make the hike down. I'd pretty much decided to return to the resort when Echo took off down the hill. I didn't see anyone or anything else suspicious. Besides, if someone was lurking around, Echo would have gone into full guard-dog mode."

"Did you notice anyone as you were walking to the cove? Maybe someone who seemed like they didn't belong?"

"No. There were people on the beach, but once I hit the trail that leads through the forest, I was completely alone. You don't think the killer watched me find the body, do you? I suppose there could have been someone watching from the top of the hill. If he was far enough away, Echo might not have noticed." The thought gave Tj chills.

"I think it's a possibility."

"So what's next?" Tj asked.

Dylan sighed. A deep, from-the-gut sigh that indicated the degree of his fatigue. "I'm heading to Reno tomorrow to see if I can figure out Tonya's movements after she got off the plane from Miami. Whatever happened occurred in a short period of time. I'm hoping I can pick something up on the airport security cameras, if nothing else."

"Is your sister still coming tomorrow?"

"So far," Dylan confirmed. "I keep waiting for her to call to say she's changed her mind. When I went to visit her in Chicago last February, things were strained between us. I'm not sure why she even agreed to the trip, except that Justin was quite adamant, and Allie really wants to make him happy."

Prior to his wife's death, Dylan had helped his sister, Allie, raise her son, and in many ways, he was more like a father to Justin than an uncle. After Dylan's wife was killed, his sister had decided spending time with Dylan was too dangerous and forbade the boy from visiting with his uncle. After the impromptu visit last winter, and a lot of negotiation on Dylan's part, Allie had agreed to come to Paradise Lake for an extended visit once Justin's school let out for the summer. Dylan hoped to talk his sister and nephew into moving to Serenity so that they could be a family once again.

"I'd like to meet her. Maybe you can bring Allie and Justin out to the resort for dinner tomorrow," Tj suggested. "It's the first day of the bikini competition, and there will be a band as well as other community events."

"Actually, I think it might be best if we wait a day or two before I take her around. Let her get comfortable at the house. I want to be sure not to overwhelm her. She's had a rough time since Anna died. In some ways, I think it affected her more than anyone else."

"Sure, no problem. Just let me know when you're ready to introduce her around. I'm excited to meet her."

Tj tried not to let the fact that Dylan didn't want her to meet his sister hurt her feelings, but she had to admit it stung. She knew how to be sensitive to the feelings of others. In fact, she was the type of person others sought out when they had a problem or needed an ear to listen or a shoulder to cry on.

"Listen, I'm sorry to be so abrupt," Dylan apologized. "It's been a long day. How about I come by for breakfast before I head to Reno tomorrow? It might be the last time we have a chance to talk for a few days."

"I'd love that."

"It'll have to be early," Dylan warned.

"Early is good with me."

"Seven?"

"See you then."

After hanging up, Tj poured the second glass of wine she'd

been pondering and returned to her place on the sofa. She pulled an afghan over her tan legs, and Cuervo crawled into her lap and began to purr. Tj closed her eyes and tried to focus on the relaxing music. Her life had changed so much in the past year. This time a year ago, she'd been a single woman with a fun and uncomplicated boyfriend, living in her own apartment in town. Then her mother died, her sisters had come to live with her, and she'd moved home to the resort. Uncomplicated, she suspected, was something that existed only in her past.

As if her life wasn't confusing enough, she decided to call the other complication in her life, ex-boyfriend Hunter Hanson. Hunter had been her boyfriend all through high school and into their first years of college. There'd been a time when she and everyone else in town had believed the two of them would marry one day. Things had been progressing decisively toward that outcome until Hunter's mother intervened, convincing him that if he wanted to be a doctor, he didn't have time to engage in such a serious relationship.

"Well, if it isn't Detective Jensen," Hunter teased when he answered his phone. Tj could picture his light blue eyes dancing with merriment as he spoke. Although he was on his way to being a respected doctor, he had a boyish quality about him that Tj hoped he'd never grow out of.

"I was just thinking about you," he added.

"Do you think about me often?" Tj teased in return.

"Always."

Her heart skipped a beat at the serious tone of Hunter's reply. She could imagine him running his hand through his thick brown hair, which he wore just a tad too long to be considered proper for an important doctor and businessman. When Hunter had first broken up with her, she'd been hurt and wanted nothing to do with him, but the pain had dulled as the years went by, and they'd managed to settle into a comfortable friendship that at times seemed to border on something more.

"The reason I called," she said, willing herself to forget about Hunter's sexy smile and focus on the task at hand, "is to check on the medical examiner's report for Tonya Overton."

"I'm not the medical examiner," Hunter pointed out.

"No, but you work at the hospital where the medical examiner works, and if I call him directly, he won't tell me anything because I don't have authorization. I'd try to get it from Dylan, but he has some personal issues on his mind. I'd prefer not to bother him."

"So you decided to bother me?"

"Exactly."

"You know I can't give you the report," Hunter said.

"No, but you might accidentally let a few details slip in casual conversation. It's the end of the day, you're tired, you don't mean to say anything, but your inhibitions are affected by the myriad of things I'm sure are marching around in your head. These things happen. No one could really blame you."

Hunter laughed. "I'm glad you called. Your seriously impaired logic has added an element of humor to what has been a truly horrendous day."

"I'm glad I could be of assistance. You have seen the report?" Tj clarified.

Tj could hear Hunter rustling paperwork on his desk "I'm looking at the report that details the preliminary findings," Hunter informed her. "We won't have a complete assessment for several days, but it doesn't seem that anything unusual or shocking has turned up at this point."

"And does the report you've managed to review confirm how Tonya died?"

Hunter hesitated.

"I found the body," Tj reminded him. "I swam down and looked into her empty eyes. I need to know she didn't suffer."

"She didn't suffer," Hunter said. "It looks as though she was hit from the side by a blunt object. Her body was placed in the water postmortem. We'll know more once we've completed a full autopsy." That confirmed what Dylan had said. "I'm sorry you had to be the one to find her. It must have been terrifying."

"I almost screamed, but I was twenty feet underwater and opening my mouth probably wouldn't be the best idea, so I swam like crazy to the surface instead. I'm pretty sure I set some kind of personal best as I made it back to shore."

"Are you going to be okay?" Hunter's voice was filled with concern.

Tj let out a long breath. "Dylan thinks the killer could still have been in the area when I arrived at the cove. I know this is crazy, but I've been worried that he saw me discover the body and might come around to tie up loose ends. Every time I hear a creak or a groan, I jump up and look around. But I know Echo would hear someone coming long before I heard anything."

"You think whoever killed Tonya might have followed you back to the resort?" Hunter asked.

"I don't know. Probably not, but you know how the mind likes to play tricks."

"I heard your dad took the girls to Disney World," Hunter said. "Is anyone there at the house with you?"

"Echo and the cats. Grandpa is out with the guys, although I don't expect him to be late. Besides, there are twenty-four models and a dozen staff members a shout away. I'm sure I'll be fine, even if there is a stalker on the loose."

"I'm just finishing up at the hospital. How about I come by and let you buy me a drink?"

"A gentleman should pay," Tj teased.

"You own the bar."

She laughed. "I'd love to have a drink with you, but I don't feel like going over to the bar. I have stuff here. Meet me at the house? Have you eaten?"

"Not yet."

"Okay, then how about I call over to the Grill and order some takeout? It should be ready by the time you get here. Any preferences?"

"A steak sounds good."

"Aren't you the one who is always lecturing everyone about cutting back on red meat?"

"Okay, then how about salmon?"

"Salmon sounds good," Tj agreed. "I was thinking that..."

"Thinking that?" Hunter prompted when Tj stopped speaking.

"Shhh. I heard something."

"Like the house settling?" Hunter asked.

"No," Tj whispered. "This was something else, and Echo is growling. Hang on."

Tj felt bad that the last thing Hunter heard before she dropped the phone and lost the connection was her bloodcurdling scream, followed by the shattering of the wineglass that had been sitting on the table next to her as it hit the wood floor.

CHAPTER 5

Thursday, June 19

"And then what happened?" Dylan laughed as Tj retold the story of what had happened the previous evening.

"I picked up a broom and shooed him out."

It turned out the late-night intruder had been a raccoon that had crawled in through an open window. Tj normally wasn't afraid of small animals, but she'd already freaked herself out with thoughts of a killer lurking in the shadows, so when the raccoon jumped out at her unexpectedly, she'd panicked. By the time she'd had the presence of mind to call Hunter back, he'd already called the sheriff's office, and her good friend, Roy Fisher, had made a trip out to the resort for nothing.

"When Roy showed up, everything was already under control." Tj giggled. "I really am sorry I didn't think to call Hunter back right away to clear things up. My main concern at the moment was to get our furry guest out of the door before the cats noticed him. Any way you deal that hand, it wasn't going to turn out well."

"I talked to Roy this morning. He said he almost had a

heart attack when Hunter called in a panic. They both expected to find you dead on the floor."

"I think I owe Hunter big-time for putting him through that. Roy too. At least you weren't on duty, so you were spared the panic."

"Yeah." Dylan sighed and leaned back. He took a sip of his coffee and stared out at the lake. Tj would give a week's pay to find out what he was thinking, but in the months she'd known Dylan, she'd learned it was better not to ask.

"It's a beautiful morning," Dylan commented as he poured his second cup of coffee, conveniently redirecting the conversation.

"It's a shame you have to go to Reno. It looks like we're in for a spectacular day. Hopefully the weather will hold. Are you excited that it's finally time for your sister's visit?"

"Honestly?" Dylan looked Tj in the eye. "I have mixed emotions. On one hand, I'm excited to see Justin. I've missed him so much. And Allie too. It's just that I know how important this visit is. If I can't convince them to move here, I've pretty much made up my mind to go back to Chicago." Dylan placed his hand over Tj's. "I've built a life in Serenity that I love. I've met people I care for and who are important to me. The thought of leaving fills me with sadness, but the idea of Justin growing up without me is unbearable."

"I'm sure Allie's going to love Paradise Lake." Tj tried for a level of certainty she was far from feeling.

"Yeah, maybe."

"The house looks fantastic. You spared no expense or effort in making both your sister and your nephew's living space warm and inviting, and the property is right on the waterfront of one of the most beautiful lakes in the country. How could she not want to stay?"

Dylan had bought a dilapidated yet large house right on the lake and spent the entire winter fixing it up. The house had six bedrooms and five bathrooms, so there was plenty of room for his sister and nephew to move in with him and his dog Kiva. It was a beautiful location, perched on the edge of an isolated cove. The beach, as all the others in the area, was considered public, but few sun-seekers bothered to make the drive to this cove, which was situated a good distance from restaurants and public facilities.

"We both know that for Allie, it's more about security than comfort," Dylan pointed out.

"I know." Tj felt tears start to form in the corners of her eyes as she stared into the flickering fire. "I suppose arriving in the middle of a murder investigation isn't exactly the situation you wanted to greet Allie with."

"I agree that the timing isn't the best. Not that the timing of a murder investigation involving such a young woman is ever the best."

"Maybe we can find the killer and wrap it up today. Your sister might never even need to hear about it. It's not like Allie knows people in town who might talk to her about it."

"Trust me when I say I know what's at stake here. But I can't lie to Allie. She'll find out about Tonya's death. I think its best that I tell her right away so she doesn't think I'm hiding things. I'm just hoping she'll fall in love with the place and look past the fact that Paradise Lake isn't immune to tragedy."

"Look at it this way," Tj said, trying her best for optimism. "You are making progress. It wasn't long ago that she didn't want you to be part of Justin's life under any circumstances. Now that you've opened the door to having a presence in his life, you just need to convince her that the life you share should be here. Piece of cake."

Dylan smiled. "I really hope so."

"I was thinking we should plan a picnic on the beach next week. Dad and the girls will be home. It might be fun to introduce Justin to Ashley. Maybe she could show him around."

Dylan hesitated. "I'll have to let you know."

"And based on what you've told me about your sister, I bet she'd love Jenna. We could invite her and her family as well."

"We'll see. I need to go. I'll call you in a few days." Dylan quickly left, even though he still had a good half hour until he needed to leave for Reno. She watched him stop to chat with her grandfather, who continued on to the Grill after Dylan walked away.

Ben poured a cup of coffee, then sat down across from Tj. "What was he in such a hurry about?"

"He's on his way to Reno to pick up his sister," Tj explained.

"Ah."

"I get the feeling he's pretty worried about how this visit will go."

"Lot at stake, I guess," Ben reasoned.

"The buffet is set up inside if you're hungry." The Tropical Tan people had ordered seasonal fruit, yogurt, egg-white omelets, and grilled salmon to be made available between seven and nine. In Tj's opinion, the brunch was a total waste as the models never seemed to eat.

"I guess I could eat. I'll make a plate in a few minutes after I have my coffee and bring it out here. It's not too bad by the fire."

"I heard we can expect afternoon temperatures in the mid-seventies all weekend," Tj informed her grandfather.

"That should make the Tropical Tan people happy."

"I didn't hear you come in last night. Late night with the guys?" Tj asked.

"Actually, I was home early. I noticed Hunter's car in the

drive, so I came in the back so as not to disturb you," Ben replied.

"It would have been fine to disturb us," Tj informed him. "I called to see if I could worm some information out of him concerning the medical examiner's report. When he realized that I was home alone after such a harrowing experience, he offered to come by to keep me company. There wasn't anything going on that couldn't be interrupted."

"There was a time you would have ranted for days if I'd walked in on your date with Hunter," Ben reminded her.

"Perhaps," Tj acknowledged. "But I'm no longer sixteen, and Hunter and I are no longer dating."

"I realize that. I guess I just continue to hope the two of you will rectify that situation. You know he still cares about you." Both Ben and Hunter's grandfather, Jake, were campaigning for them to reunite and provide them with great-grandbabies.

"He broke up with me," Tj reminded him.

"That was a long time ago. Things have changed. You've both changed."

"I know," Tj said. "I love Hunter. I've always loved Hunter. But things aren't as simple as you and Jake want to make them."

"Perhaps you're right." Ben placed his hand over Tj's. "Any word on the missing model?"

"Not so far."

"Normally, I wouldn't be overly concerned, since she seems to have left on her own terms, but after what happened to Tonya Overton..."

"Yeah, I'm worried too," Tj said. "I thought I'd go into town and show her photo around. If she's still in the area, someone must have seen her."

"She does look familiar," Ben said.

"Her bio lists Serenity as her hometown," Tj informed him.

"She didn't go through our school system or I'd know her, so I'm guessing she only moved to the area recently or was homeschooled."

"More and more folks doing that these days."

"I thought I'd show Jenna her photo. I need to go by the Antiquery to pick up the cookies she made for the snack bar. She sees a lot of people come through the restaurant."

"Sounds like a good idea. And as long as you're at the Antiquery, maybe you can put one of the help-wanted flyers I worked up on the community bulletin board. The resort is almost booked solid for the summer, so I thought we might need to hire some extra help."

"Dad said something about that before he left. I can put some ads out to social media sites if you want."

"Guess you should wait to talk to your dad about it when he gets back from Florida."

"I hope the girls are having fun at Disney World. I was thinking I'd call them when I'm done eating. They've only been gone one day and I already miss them so much."

Ben stood up. "Give them my love. I think I'll skip the buffet and head over to make sure things are ready for the Tropical Tan staff. I guess they plan to tell the models about Tonya when they arrive. I figured I'd set something up in the activities room."

Tj watched her grandfather walk away. She was debating the timing of her call to the East Coast to speak with her sisters when Amber walked up and nervously stood in front of her.

"Good morning, Amber."

"Mornin', Miss Tj."

"Just Tj."

"Uh, sure."

"Did you need something?" Tj waited as Amber fidgeted

around, trying to work up the courage to tell her something.

"If'n you hear something that someone said, but they don't know you heard them say it, is it gossipin' if you tell what you heard to someone else?"

"Probably," Tj answered. "Please have a seat." She motioned to the chair Ben had just vacated. "Why don't you tell me what you heard, and then we'll decide if it's something that should be told."

"It's about the missin' girl."

"Kiara?" Tj asked.

"No. The one who was supposed to be on the bus."

"Tonya Overton?"

"Yes, ma'am. I was helpin' to clear tables in the bar last night while the models were there. I overheard a group of them sayin' that Ms. Overton had gotten herself into big trouble when the tour stopped in Las Vegas a while back. They made it sound like she lost a lot of money gamblin' and was havin' a hard time payin' back these dangerous people. One of the models said Ms. Overton probably missed the bus 'cause she was chasin' after a royal flush. They suggested that you might look for her in one of the casinos."

It was way too late for that, but Tj wasn't at liberty to tell Amber or anyone else what had actually happened to Tonya. Still, Tonya's gambling addiction and subsequent debt was something Dylan would be interested to know. "Thank you for telling me what you heard." Tj placed her hand over Amber's. "Normally, repeating things we overhear isn't a good thing to do, but in this case it might help us to understand what happened to Tonya. I'll be sure to pass this information along to the sheriff's department."

Amber stood up. "Thank you, ma'am. I hope you find her and she's okay."

Tj watched Amber walk away. Tonya's gambling problem could turn out to be a significant clue. While there was a limited amount of gambling in the family town of Serenity, several of the larger casinos in Indulgence, on the south end of the lake, were known to be run by people involved in organized crime. What if Tonya had gotten in too deep with the wrong person? Of course, if she headed to a casino in Reno or Indulgence, it didn't explain how she'd ended up in Secret Cove. Chances were her death had to do with something else entirely, though she supposed it couldn't hurt to mention what Amber had told her to Dylan the next time she spoke to him.

Tj finished the last of her coffee and was gathering her things when her cell rang. "Hi, Dad."

"It's not Papa, it's Gracie," her youngest sister giggled.

"Hi, baby. How's Disney World?" Tj felt her heart swell with love at the sound of the little girl's voice.

"So, so fun. I went on lots of rides and got to see Minnie Mouse."

"You've already been on rides?"

"We got here when they opened," Gracie verified. Tj glanced at her watch. It was after nine. She hadn't realized she'd been sitting there that long. With the time change, it must be lunch time in Florida. "Ashley was scared of the teacups, but Rosalie and I went on them two times."

"I wasn't scared," Tj heard Ashley yell.

"Ashley gets motion sickness, like Mom used to," Tj reminded her sister. "I'm sure she just didn't want to get a queasy stomach. Are you at the park right now?"

"Yeah. Miss Rosalie brought us 'cause Papa had to work. He's going to meet us later."

"It's my turn to talk," Ashley insisted in the background.

"It's still my turn," Gracie replied.

"You guys can argue later," Tj interrupted after the exchange threatened to exclude her entirely. "Did you see the princesses?"

"Not yet. I want to see Belle and Ashley wants to see Ariel. Papa says we can get dresses to bring home. Does Crissy miss me?" Gracie asked.

"She does, but she decided to sleep with me while you're gone. Cuervo wasn't real happy about that, but the two have come to an agreement, I think."

"I wish we could have brought her."

"I don't think they allow cats in Disney World."

"I seen a dog."

"It was probably a service dog," Tj explained.

"Your time is up." Tj heard a scuffle as the girls fought over the phone. Rosalie said something that seemed to end the tussle, and Gracie came back on the line.

"Ashley wants to say hi, and Miss Rosalie said I have to share."

"I think that's a good idea. I miss you bunches."

"I miss you bunches too."

"Remember who loves you the most."

"You do." Gracie giggled.

So much had changed in Tj's life in the past year. Before the girls came to live with her the previous July, having kids was the furthest thing from her mind. She'd always considered herself to be one of those people who would do just as well without tiny mini-mes hanging on her arm or wiping their nose on her pant leg. But now that she'd experienced the joy of mini-mes, nose wiping and all, she didn't know what she'd do without them.

"Hi, Tj." Ashley came on the line.

"Hi yourself. Are you having fun?"

"So much fun," Ashley confirmed. "I want to go on the

roller coaster, but Gracie is too little. Rosalie said I have to wait until Papa meets us, so one of them can go with me and one of them can wait with her."

"That sounds like a good plan. Have you been on some of the other rides?"

"Lots. Papa got a special pass and we got to go to the front of the line. My favorite was the Pirates of the Caribbean. There was real fire and real cannons."

"Sounds awesome. I'm sorry I couldn't come."

"Me too. It would have been much more fun if you were here. We could go on the biggest roller coaster together."

"Maybe next time."

"We're going to have lunch right now, so I guess I should hang up."

"If you have Papa's phone, what phone does he have?" Tj wondered. When Gracie had called, the caller ID clearly indicated that she was calling from her father's phone.

"He has Rosalie's. His phone was out of batteries when he had to leave this morning 'cause he forgot to charge it, so they traded so Rosalie could charge his for him. They're going to trade back when he meets us later. We're supposed to let any calls go to voicemail."

"I see. Can I talk to Rosalie for a minute before you hang up?"

"Sure, hang on."

Tj waited while Ashley transferred the phone to Rosalie. When Tj had made the decision to remain behind in order to help Ben with the Tropical Tan group, it had seemed like a good idea. Now, as she listened to their laughter in the background, she found herself regretting her decision. Ben had run the resort without any help for over twenty-five years. Now that her dad had taken over, Tj had begun to think of her grandpa as less than capable, but the truth of the matter was that he was still able to run the resort or do anything else he set his mind to.

"How are things with the models?" Rosalie asked.

"Interesting. How is Disney World?"

"I'm having the best time with Ashley and Gracie. Who knew kids could be so great?"

Rosalie was the town veterinarian. She was popular and had a lot of friends, but she'd never married or had any children of her own. She was quite a bit younger than her father and so still able to have children someday if she chose. Tj wondered if there might be another half-sister in her future.

CHAPTER 6

After she finished talking to Rosalie, Tj headed into town. She had told Connor she'd try to make it to the choir rehearsal, and although she was over an hour late, she figured she could catch the end to show her support.

When she walked into the community center, Connor was doing a duet with a shy sophomore who Tj had figured had no chance of contributing to the choir when she first met her. Kendall had not only blossomed under Kyle's tutelage but had ended up being one of the better singers. Tj slipped into a chair in the back of the room as the medley of patriotic songs continued.

"They're really good," Pastor Dan Kensington said as he slipped into the chair beside her. Dan had moved to Serenity with his three-year-old daughter Hannah after his wife died. At thirty-five, he was a lot younger than the elderly pastor he'd replaced.

"I know. I'm as amazed as anyone," Tj whispered. "Have you been here long?"

"A few minutes. I want to talk to Kendall and a few of the others about joining the church choir. I was waiting backstage for the kids to finish, but I saw you come in and decided to wait with you instead."

"I'm glad you did. It's been a while since we've run into each other."

"I noticed you haven't been to services in a while."

"Yeah." Tj blushed. It was dark in the room, so Tj hoped Dan couldn't see the guilt on her face. "I guess I've been busy."

"I went by the hospital yesterday to visit with Mrs. Roberson." Mrs. Roberson had been sick for quite some time, and Dan went by at least three times a week to sit with her. "I ran into Hunter, and he told me about the woman you found in the cove. I don't suppose you have any word on her next of kin? I'd like to offer my services if they're in need of support."

"No," Tj whispered. "I haven't heard anything. I guess you can check with Roy. He's in charge while Dylan is on leave."

"I did stop by the sheriff's office last night when I finished sitting with Mrs. Roberson, but the woman at the desk said Roy was out on a call."

Tj blushed again. "That was me."

Dan frowned. "Is everything okay?"

"Yeah, everything is fine. The intruder turned out to be a raccoon. I don't suppose you can keep this to yourself? It's kind of embarrassing. I'd hate to see my reputation as a tough guy take a hit."

Dan laughed. "Your secret is safe with me. You might check in with Jenna, though. She peeked in a while ago, and I asked her about the 911 call to the resort. She looked worried."

"Yeah, I will." Tj looked at her watch. She had a lot to do that day, and she really should talk to Jenna before she totally freaked out about the incident the evening before. "I need to get going. It was nice talking to you. Can you let Connor and the kids know I was here, and they sound great?"

* * *

Like all the other storefronts on Main Street, the sidewalk space in front of the Antiquery was decked out with barrels of flowers in every color imaginable. The Antiquery was a popular establishment, combining home-style dining with antiques that Jenna's mother, Helen, managed to dig up by attending estate sales in the area.

Tj parked in the alley behind the eatery and went in through the back door, which led directly into the kitchen, where Jenna could normally be found between the hours of seven and two.

"I heard about the dispatch to the resort last night. What happened?" Jenna, tall and thin, with light blue eyes and long blond hair twisted into a braid, greeted her. Jenna had been Tj's best friend since preschool.

"Raccoon in the kitchen."

Jenna laughed. "Since when are you scared of raccoons?"

"I'm not. It was just a misunderstanding. I was on the phone with Hunter." Tj filled Jenna in on the entire fiasco.

"That's hilarious. I'm glad you came by. I was getting worried, although I guess you could have just called and saved yourself the trip."

"I ran into Dan at the community center and he told me you'd talked. I figured I should head over to explain. Besides, I wanted to pick up the cookies you made for the snack bar, and I need to put up one of these on your bulletin board." Tj held up the help-wanted flyer her grandpa had given her.

"There are tacks in the board," Jenna informed her. "Just stick it wherever you want."

"I'll do it before I leave." Tj slid onto one of the stools lining the counter. "Did Dennis and the girls leave on their trip yet?"

Jenna's firefighter husband had a long weekend off and planned to take their two daughters camping.

"Yeah, they left this morning. At first I was sorry it wasn't going to work out for me to go with them, but now I find that I'm looking forward to a few days to myself."

"We have bands on the beach all weekend. I can have someone reserve one of the fire pits and we can drink wine, eat cheese, and listen to the music under the stars." While open fires weren't allowed in the area due to fire restrictions, fires built within a pit were permitted during all but the driest of years. The resort provided forest service-approved pits in both the campground and on the beach bordering the resort. The pits were generally considered first come, first served, but Tj could usually manage to have one of her staff reserve one if she made the request early enough in the day.

"Sounds perfect," Jenna agreed. "How are things going at the resort with your dad out of town?"

"Except for the missing model and the murdered Tropical Tan employee, not bad."

"What?" Jenna stopped what she was doing. "Murdered employee?"

"I shouldn't have said anything, so you have to promise to keep this to yourself."

"Yeah, no problem. What's going on?"

Tj explained about looking for Kiara and finding Tonya's body in the process.

"I can't believe you found another body. What is that, three in eight months?"

"I know. It's like I'm cursed. There's isn't much I can do to help Tonya. Dylan is looking into her death. Still, I would like to find Kiara. It doesn't make sense that she'd work so hard to make it to the final twenty-five and then just take off when her dream of winning the scholarship the other models tell me she was desperate to have was so close."

"You think something happened to her?" Jenna asked.

"I think there's a good possibility that foul play is involved in her disappearance. The girl is from Serenity. Or at least she listed Serenity as her hometown on her bio. Do you recognize her?"

Jenna wiped her hands on a dish towel and took the photo from Tj. "You know, she does look familiar." Jenna bit her lip as she continued to study the photo. "I'm trying to remember where I've seen her."

"This photo is a professionally snapped headshot, so you might need to picture her with ?   ; makeup and maybe more casual hair."

"It seems like if she's from here, you'd know who she is. She looks like a teenager."

"She's eighteen," Tj verified. "I'm certain she didn't go through our school system. I'm guessing she was homeschooled. On the day she went missing, a girl who I guess is twelve or thirteen came looking for her. She said she was Kiara's half-sister. Her name is Annabeth."

"Doesn't sound familiar. You know, this girl could be the same one I used to see in the library from time to time. I never spoke to her, but I remember seeing a girl with similar features reading in a corner when I visited a time or two. Why don't you ask Frannie if she knows who she is?"

CHAPTER 7

Jenna's suggestion that Frannie Edison might know Kiara was the only lead Tj had, so after she finished her conversation with Jenna, grabbed the cookies, and hung the flyer on the bulletin board, she headed down the street toward the town and county buildings. The library was one of Tj's favorite places. Built as a bordello at the turn of the century, it had been converted into a library more than sixty years earlier, a few years after the town was incorporated. The downstairs, which at one time had served as a common room for entertaining, held a large wooden counter that was now used as a reference desk but originally served as the bar on which girls had danced to entertain the men. Behind the counter were rows of bookshelves holding reference materials that could only be accessed with librarian supervision. In front of the counter was an open area in which round tables surrounded by chairs were provided for patrons. The upstairs was divided into smaller rooms, converted from bedrooms into bookrooms, each with its own subject matter. One room was decorated in nursery rhymes and held children's books, another housed fiction, yet another reference and business books, and another self-help and religion. Each bookroom contained long sofas or cozy chairs for visitors who wished to preview a book before checking it out and taking it home.

"Afternoon, Tj," Frannie said when Tj walked through the front door. Frannie stood behind the counter, where she was checking in a new shipment of books. "Isn't it a beautiful day?"

"It really is," Tj agreed. "In fact, I think this is one of the nicest Junes we've had in quite a few years."

"The timing of the warm weather is perfect for the long weekend. How are you doing with the models this year?" Frannie asked.

"I'm actually here because one of them never checked in," Tj informed Frannie. "Do you know this girl?"

Frannie took the photo from Tj. "Yeah, I know her. Her name is Kiara Boswell. She used to come in to check out books every other day before she left the area."

"Do you know if she has family in town?"

"Kiara didn't live in Serenity. She lived in Vengeance."

"Which would explain why she didn't go to school in our system," Tj realized.

It made sense that Kiara listed Serenity rather than Vengeance as her hometown. Vengeance was a village about five miles north of Paradise Lake. The area had been settled by isolationists who'd chosen to live off the grid. The only access to the small village was a rutted dirt road that wound up the mountain several miles after leaving the highway. Most children were homeschooled, and exposure to the outside world was discouraged, if not forbidden, by many of the families who resided there.

"Did she ever talk about friends in town? Perhaps a boyfriend?"

Tj waited while Frannie considered her question. "No, not that I can remember. Kiara mostly kept to herself. She loved to read. I think she found books to be the only friend she needed. I do know she was unhappy living in such isolation and wanted very badly to go to college. I wasn't surprised when she left."

"Did you know she entered the Ms. Tropical Tan contest?"

Frannie looked both shocked and pleased, her bright green eyes lighting up as she answered. "No, I didn't know. Good for her. You said she never checked in?"

"She's missing." Tj explained about the events that occurred after the bus from Reno had arrived, leaving out the part about the dead woman in the cove since Dylan hadn't given her the go-ahead to talk about that yet. "Do you recognize this man?" Tj handed her Doc's sketch.

Frannie studied it. Her brows furrowed beneath the medium brown bangs that framed her face. "No, I can't say that I do. This is the man she left with?"

"According to the other models, this is what he looked like. The sketch is a composite of the descriptions we received."

"Do you think Kiara is in some kind of trouble?" Frannie asked.

"We're not sure. The girls reported that Kiara seemed to leave with the man willingly, so we're operating under the assumption that she knew him. Perhaps he was a boyfriend or even a brother."

"Kiara never mentioned a boyfriend. Honestly, in all the years I knew her, I never saw her speak to anyone other than her grandmother, who used to drop her off and then return for her an hour or so later. Do you think the man Kiara left with is from the village?"

"We don't know at this point," Tj informed her. "I suppose I could go out to the compound and see what I can find out."

"They won't let you past the gate at the end of the road," Frannie warned her. "The compound is on private property, and the privacy of the villagers is well guarded."

"Do you think they're dangerous?" Tj asked.

Frannie considered this. "Dangerous? Probably not. But the people who have chosen to settle in that remote location have done so for a reason. I believe Kiara might have descended from the original family that settled in the area, but there are others who choose to live there for different reasons."

Tj realized Frannie was correct in her assumption that she'd never make it past the front gate. She needed to find someone in the village who knew Kiara and might be able to provide her current whereabouts. "Can you think of anyone who might know if Kiara has friends or family I can talk to?"

"Not really, although you might talk to Hazel."

"Hazel?" Tj asked. Hazel Whipple was the seventy-two-year-old postmistress who, everyone agreed, should have retired years ago.

"Kiara's grandmother would often go visit with Hazel while she waited for Kiara to finish up here, so they must be friends of a sort. If Hazel can get a message to the grandmother, she might be able to help you with your search."

"I'll head to the post office next. Did Kiara ever mention why she left the area?"

"Not specifically. I know she was having issues with her dad, and that she wanted to go to college more than anything. She's a bright girl with a keen mind who deserves to have a chance at a life outside of Vengeance. My guess is that her father wouldn't let her go away to school, so she ran away."

That fit what the other models had said about Kiara joining the competition for the scholarship.

"Okay, thanks. If you think of or hear anything, call me."

"I will. And please let me know when you find her," Frannie added. "I grew fond of the girl over the years. We didn't speak often, but there was something about her serene nature and quiet focus that I identified with."

* * *

"You need to gain control over those models of yours," Hazel said the moment Tj walked through the door.

Hazel Whipple ran a tight ship. She'd been working at the post office in Serenity since there'd been a post office. Hazel, who always wore a proper shin-length day dress and sturdy one-inch heels, was feistier than most women half her age. Technically, she should have retired from the post office with a full pension years earlier, but the spunky widow was determined to remain employed until they put her in a pine box, a sentiment she often shared when concerned friends tried to talk her into slowing down. She'd never had children and her husband had died more than thirty years ago. Most felt that, as far as Hazel was concerned, the post office, which had been a constant in her life for more than fifty years, was the only family she had left.

"Has there been a problem?"

"You bet there's been a problem." Hazel's eyes flashed in annoyance. "One of those trollops you're harboring at the resort had the nerve to come into my post office wearing nothing but a pair of shorts and a bathing suit top. The sign on the front door specifically states that both shirts and shoes must be worn in this establishment at all times."

"That's true, but this is a beach town, and most of the businesses loosen the rules during bikini season."

"Well, this establishment is not one of those places, and the rule is nonnegotiable. Just because we have a beach nearby doesn't mean we have to live like heathens. The girl had bare feet, shorts so short as to be indecent, and a barely concealed bosom. I told the woman she would need to come back later wearing proper attire if she wanted me to post her package. She tried to argue, but the rules are the rules, and if we choose to ignore them, it won't be long before society as a whole leans toward anarchy."

Tj figured she'd get an earful from whichever model was turned away when she got back to the resort. Hazel was a strong woman who could be a wonderful and supportive friend, but at times her ideals were so completely outdated that many thought they bordered on the absurd.

"The reason I'm here is because I'm looking for this girl." Tj handed Hazel the photo. "Do you know her?"

"Of course I know her. I make it my business to know everyone."

"Fantastic." Tj was trying hard to hold her temper with the cranky woman. Hazel hadn't always been as snarky as she'd been lately; it seemed the aches and pains associated with her advancing age had turned a proper but polite woman into a bitter old lady. "Have you seen her in the past day or two?"

"I haven't seen her in over a year. She moved away, from what I've been told."

"She's part of the group from the Tropical Tan contest," Tj informed her. "She came up the mountain with the other models yesterday, but no one has seen her since. I'm trying to get hold of anyone who might know of her whereabouts. I understand you know her grandmother."

"Nona Cooper." Hazel nodded.

"Do you have a way of getting in touch with her?"

"You say Kiara was with those models?" Hazel frowned. Whereas Frannie had a look of delight when she'd learned Kiara had gotten away from her strict upbringing to do something new, Hazel obviously disapproved of the girl's choice.

"Yes, ma'am. She was doing quite well. After months of preliminary competitions, she was chosen as part of the final twenty-five. It's really quite an accomplishment."

"And she left after she arrived?" Hazel clarified.

"Yes. She left with this man after the bus arrived." Tj handed Hazel the sketch Doc had drawn of the man who met Kiara at the bus.

"Aaron," Hazel stated with certainty.

"Aaron?"

"Her fiancé," Hazel informed Tj.

"I wasn't aware Kiara was engaged." The truth of the matter was that not one piece of information Tj had gained since the models had arrived suggested Kiara was engaged.

"Nona told me Kiara wasn't keen on the arrangement. I don't have all the details, but I believe it was something her father agreed to with another man in the village."

"Kiara was in an arranged engagement?"

"Apparently."

"No wonder she left the area. Do you think you can set up a meeting for me with Nona?" Tj asked.

"Nona is particular about who she speaks to. I doubt she'd want to talk to you, although she does know your grandpa and might be willing to talk to him. I suppose I could set up a meeting with both of you, if Ben is willing."

"Grandpa knows Nona?"

"They play bingo together."

"Bingo?"

"At the senior center. Nona likes to get away from Vengeance from time to time, so she plays bingo. Nona doesn't get along with many people from town, but she seems to like your grandpa all right. If you want to talk to her, you'll need to do so through Ben, although I doubt Nona will support any idea you may have of trying to get Kiara to come back to the competition."

"I'm not here to try to talk Kiara into changing her mind if she's decided not to follow through on the contest. I just want to make sure she's okay."

"Why wouldn't she be okay?" Hazel asked.

Tj hesitated. She wasn't supposed to talk about Tonya, but her death might be the leverage she needed to get Hazel's cooperation.

"I need to tell you something, but you have to promise to keep it to yourself."

"Of course. I'm not a gossip."

Tj wasn't sure about that. It seemed that Hazel was more often than not in the thick of things if there was something of importance to be known and communicated. She wasn't quite as bad as Jenna's mother, Helen, who was the self-appointed queen bee of the local gossip hotline, but Tj was taking a risk by letting Hazel in on a secret Dylan had warned her not to share. On the other hand, now that the Tropical Tan staff had informed the models of Tonya's death, Tj was fairly certain that word of the murder would be common knowledge by the end of the day.

"There was another missing girl," Tj began. "She's dead."

CHAPTER 8

By the time Tj got back to the resort, the contestants were gathered on the beach modeling swimwear for a photoshoot. The Tropical Tan staff had arrived and informed the models of Tonya Overton's death. Tj headed to the house to check on the animals before heading to the beach to watch the models pose in various positions on the sand and in the water.

"Roy, what are you doing here?" Tj asked the deputy, who was in charge now that Dylan was officially on leave.

"Following up on a lead. At least I'm trying to figure out how to follow up. I hate to admit it, but I don't have the training for something like this."

Prior to Dylan's arrival the previous fall, the town of Serenity had seen very few murders. Roy had been on the force for quite a while but didn't have Dylan's expertise in investigating serious crime. The other local deputy, Tim Matthews, had even less experience than Roy.

"What sort of lead?" Tj asked.

Roy hesitated.

"Come on, Roy. You know you can trust me. What lead?"

Tj had helped the sheriff's department solve two murders to date, so Tj figured Roy had reason to trust her instincts. Besides, why would he be standing around hoping to run into her if he hadn't already decided he wanted her help?

"We managed to speak on the phone to Tonya's old

roommate. After she got the job with Tropical Tan, Tonya rented a house with two other women for a short time. One of the women, Alexandra Dolby, still lives in the house the three women shared, and we managed to track her down. According to Alexandra, Tonya was messing around with Fenton Ridley during the first few months she was employed by his company."

Tj looked toward the beach, where Fenton and a handful of Tropical Tan staff were watching the photoshoot. Fenton was not only making all the calls, but he was the primary owner of the Tropical Tan Corporation.

"They were having an affair?" Tj clarified.

"If Tonya's ex-roommate can be believed. According to Alexandra, the affair was as brief as it was intense, and Fenton broke things off after a couple of months."

"Okay." Tj attempted to wrap her head around this piece of information. Fenton Ridley was not only filthy rich but gorgeous as well. In addition to that, he was married and had been for quite some time. "I guess I can see that the situation was delicate, but how does that make him a suspect?"

"I didn't say he was a suspect," Roy pointed out. "I said that the information I received was a lead. It seems the affair ended badly. Alexandra told me Tonya was extremely angry when they broke up and threatened to tell his wife."

"Which gives him a motive for murder," I said.

"Exactly."

"Yeah, but why now?" Tj asked. "If Tonya and Fenton were sleeping together and he broke if off a while back, why would Fenton kill Tonya now? She'd been working for the company for a year, so wouldn't the affair be old news?"

"Opportunity?" Roy took a stab.

"Except for the fact that the Tropical Tan staff didn't arrive until this morning and Tonya was killed yesterday."

"I checked the flight the majority of the Tropical Tan staff arrived on this morning. Neither Fenton nor his wife were listed as passengers," Roy informed her. "Fenton, his wife, his wife's sister, and his son from a previous marriage all flew in on a private jet. His party arrived yesterday morning. I confirmed that all four members of the party checked into the Serenity Lodge at eleven a.m. The affair, coupled with the opportunity, makes Fenton a person of interest at the very least."

"So bring him into the station and interview him," Tj suggested.

"Sheriff Boggs says no. He says we have nothing to go on, and he doesn't want to bother someone with Fenton's wealth and influence unless we can come up with more."

Typical Boggs. Always looking out for his reputation.

"Okay, I get what you're saying." Tj turned to face Roy. "It seems like a long shot, but I guess it wouldn't hurt to dig around. What's your plan?"

"Plan?"

"You're here in your uniform. I figured you had a plan."

Roy sighed. "Showing up and scouting out the situation was as far as I got. Boggs basically forbid me from interviewing the man, but maybe you can chat with Fenton and see what you can find out."

Tj glanced back toward the photoshoot. In addition to Fenton and the photographer, there were three hairstylists, two makeup artists, and five Tropical Tan employees assisting with props and bathing suit changes. It would be difficult to strike up a casual conversation.

"The photoshoot should be close to wrapping up," Tj informed Roy. "I haven't had a chance to speak to Fenton since he arrived. When they're done, I'll suggest we get a drink or a bite to eat so we can discuss the accommodations and any special instructions he may have for our staff. I can't guarantee anything, but I'll try to steer the conversation where you need it to go. What do you want me to find out exactly?"

"I don't know. Talk to him about Tonya. See if you can get him to say anything about his feelings about her death. I doubt he'll come right out and admit they had an affair, but you might be able to get a feel for their relationship."

"Okay." Tj looked at her watch. "I need to run over and talk to Grandpa. I'm hoping he can set up a meeting with Kiara's grandmother for this evening. After I do that, I'll come by again to talk to Fenton. It's probably best that you're out of sight. The last thing we need is for him to realize he's a person of interest. He'll clam up for sure."

Roy nodded. "I'm going to see if I can find out some more about his wife and the rest of his party. Call me after you speak to him."

Fenton said he'd be delighted to have a drink. The bar was crowded, but Tj managed to secure a spot out on the deck. Fortunately, Logan Cole was working the outdoor bar. She had an agreement with her beverage manager to skip the rum if she ordered a Mai Tai when she was with a customer. That provided a way to enjoy the social convention of having a drink without succumbing to the effects of alcohol. More often than not, this gave her an upper hand in steering the conversation.

"How are you enjoying your trip so far?" Tj asked. She nibbled on the maraschino cherry sitting atop the colorful drink she'd ordered.

"It's been challenging," Fenton admitted after downing a shot of their finest scotch. "Having to tell the models what happened to Tonya wasn't easy."

"I can imagine that. Is there anything my staff or I can do to make things easier on you and your people?"

Tj motioned for Logan to refill Fenton's drink.

"No. You've all been great, and the accommodations you've provided are perfect, as usual."

"I understand you aren't staying with us this year."

Fenton looked surprised that she knew about it but recovered quickly. "My wife and son and my wife's sister all decided to tag along. I figured it would be best not to have her underfoot while I was working, so we rented rooms in town."

"Is your wife able to travel with you often?" Tj took a small sip of her drink as she waited for Fenton to answer.

"Occasionally."

He seemed guarded in his answers. If Tj had to guess, Fenton was less than thrilled with his wife's presence. He was a nice-looking man who probably had no trouble finding companionship during his time away from home. He looked like he was in his late forties to early fifties, which made him quite a bit older than the models and staff he traveled with, but he'd managed to maintain his playboy looks, and his photograph appeared frequently in the tabloids with a variety of women.

"I imagine it's nice to have her with you for support after what happened to Tonya. It must have been quite a shock to find out that one of your employees had been murdered."

"Tonya was special. One of my best employees in fact. The girls loved her. She'll be missed," he added with a catch in his voice.

Fenton looked and sounded sincere. He downed his second shot, which Logan immediately refilled.

"I overheard one of the girls mention that the two of you were close," Tj fished.

"We worked together for over a year. During that time, we

got to know each other fairly well, although I wouldn't say I was closer to her than to any of my other employees. When you travel as part of your job, you tend to form close relationships with the people on your team. I enjoy spending time with my employees, and they seem to enjoy spending time with me. We have fun together."

"Maybe, but I'm sure all that travel is hard on your wife, as well as Tonya's boyfriend."

"My wife doesn't seem to mind, and Tonya didn't have a boyfriend. At least not one I knew of. My assistant, Tony, has a hard time with the travel, however. His wife is expecting their first child, so Tony has decided to hang it up after this competition. It's hard to be a dad if you're never around."

"You mentioned your son is with you. Do you have other children?"

Fenton downed his third shot. "No. Porter is my child from my first marriage."

"I seem to remember reading something about him in one of those gossip blogs that seem to be everywhere these days. You weren't close until recently?"

Fenton downed another shot.

"I was a horrible husband and father because I was never home, which is why I understand where Tony is coming from. My current wife travels a lot herself, and since we don't have children, she doesn't seem to mind the long separations." Fenton frowned. "I don't know why I'm telling you all of this."

Tj laughed. "People say I'm easy to talk to." And you're half sloshed, Tj thought but didn't say as much.

"Yeah, I guess you are. Too bad you aren't looking for a job; you'd be just the type of person who would be fun to go on the road with."

"Personally, I'd hate all that travel. I'm a bit of a homebody.

I didn't know Tonya well, but she seemed to find the travel tedious as well."

"Really? Why do you say that?"

"I don't know. Just an impression I got when we spoke. I suppose I could have caught her at a moment when she was missing her family."

Fenton motioned for another glass of scotch. Tj instructed Logan to leave the bottle. The more Fenton drank, the more he talked.

"Tonya didn't seem to have any family to miss," Fenton said after he downed the scotch and refilled his glass. "I know she seemed lonely and disconnected when we were in Miami for long periods of time. We had dinner a few times, and she indicated she didn't have much to go home to."

"So she didn't have any close friends outside of work?"

"Not that I know of. Tonya was very focused on her job. That's what made her such a good employee. She was always willing to work as many hours as we needed her. If she had lived, I'm certain she would have had a bright future with Tropical Tan."

"And she never mentioned a love interest?"

Fenton looked at Tj. "I believe I just said that."

"I'm sorry, I guess you did. It seems I remember someone mentioning she was involved in an affair a while back."

Fenton shrugged. "If she was, she didn't talk to me about it."

He drank another shot of the whiskey. Tj didn't know how he did it. She'd be passed out on the floor if she drank as much as he had, but he wasn't even slurring his words.

"I guess you know that the sheriff's office is beginning the process of speaking to everyone who knew Tonya."

Tj watched Fenton's face.

He didn't even flinch. "Makes sense. They want to figure out who did this terrible thing."

"I guess so. I imagine they'll be looking into Tonya's past relationships. Friends, family, lovers," Tj offered. "They may even want to speak to you and the models, since you seemed to know her best."

"I'd be happy to talk to them, and I'll instruct my staff to do so as well if it will help, but I'll request that they work around the schedule we've already set up," Fenton said. "It's hard enough to maintain an atmosphere of business as usual with Tonya's death and Kiara's disappearance on everyone's mind." Fenton took out his phone and consulted his calendar. "First thing in the morning would be best for me. Should I call the sheriff's office, or will you inform them?"

Tj hesitated.

"I noticed you speaking to the deputy earlier and assume that's the motivation behind the scotch and this very lovely conversation?"

CHAPTER 9

Ben was not only successful in getting Nona to meet them but agreed to go with Tj while she spoke to her as well. The drive out of town to the location where the meeting had been arranged would take about twenty minutes from the resort. Ben had gone down to the beach where Doc was entered into the home brewing competition; leave it to Doc to be cooking something up if there was something to be cooked. Tj had tasted the beer from some of Doc's early batches and hoped he'd made quite a lot of progress in the craft.

"How's it going?" Tj asked Doc when she'd made her way down to the beach.

"I made it into the final round," Doc announced proudly. "Have a taste."

He handed her a small glass of the dark brew. Tj tentatively took a sip "This is really good."

"You sound surprised," Doc teased.

"Not surprised," Tj said, trying to cover. "Just…"

"Don't worry. I tasted the first few batches I made and realized they were pretty awful."

"Practice makes perfect." Tj took another sip. "What is that flavor? It's sort of fruity."

"Peach," Doc answered. "I call it fuzzy peach ale."

"It's excellent. I hope you have more to share."

"Of course. I thought I'd bring some when I come over for the next poker game with the guys. I'll be sure to bring you a bottle."

"Thanks, I'd like that." Tj looked around. "There's a lot better turnout than I expected."

"Home brewing has become a popular pastime," Doc explained. "If you have time, you should make the rounds and taste some of the other entries."

Tj looked at the more than twenty booths that had been set up for tasting. If she didn't need to leave, it would be fun to sample all the different blends.

"Grandpa and I are on our way to talk with Kiara's grandmother about her disappearance, but maybe if everyone is still around when we get back, I'll taste a few. Are you ready?" Tj asked Ben.

"Yeah. I guess we should be going. I'd hate to keep Nona waiting."

"I'll be here a couple more hours at least," Doc told them. "Why don't you come back by after your talk? We can listen to some music and have a bite to eat."

"Sounds good to me," Ben replied.

"If I'm not here, meet me by the bandstand," Doc said. "If you don't see me right away, text me. I have my phone."

"Okay. See you in a bit. And good luck with the competition," Ben added.

"Yeah, good luck." Tj hugged the older man, who, as usual, was dressed in his signature Hawaiian shirt.

"Hazel mentioned that you met Nona through the senior center," Tj said as she and Ben walked back toward the parking area.

"I first met Nona through your grandmother." Ben waved to

some of the other seniors he socialized with as they passed the bandstand.

"Grandma knew Nona?" Tj asked. Her grandmother had been dead for several years, so Tj was surprised to hear that she knew the mysterious woman.

"They met before I even knew your grandmother," Ben confirmed. "Maggie's family summered at Paradise Lake from the time she was a child. Nona moved to the area after her parents were killed in an accident and she was sent to live with her uncle. I think she was a teenager at the time."

"The uncle lived in Vengeance?"

"Actually, the uncle lived in Serenity," Ben said as he climbed into the passenger side of the vehicle. "According to what Maggie told me, Nona didn't move to Vengeance until after she was an adult. She didn't get along with the other teens in the area and tended to keep to herself. When Maggie ran into Nona in town during one of the summers she spent at the lake, she decided to take her on as a project."

"Project?"

"You know your grandmother." Ben laughed. "She was a social whirlwind who didn't like to see people alone. She saw herself as some sort of social messiah whose mission was to bully people out of their shells."

"Which is exactly how the two of you got together," Tj said.

"That it was." Ben smiled fondly.

When her grandfather first met her grandmother, they hadn't gotten along. All her grandfather wanted was to be left alone on the isolated parcel of land he'd purchased with an inheritance.

Maggie, on the other hand, was a five-foot-tall spitfire who insisted on hanging around and giving Ben advice he claimed he didn't want or need. By the end of the summer, they were hopelessly in love and were married in the little church in Serenity before the first snow fell.

"Back to Nona...I take it that Grandma was successful in bringing her into the social fold?"

"Not exactly. I guess Nona was fourteen or fifteen when she moved here. She had an unsettling way about her. The combination of her sharp mind and keen sense of observation coupled with a total lack of social skills caused her to make comments that people found off-putting."

"Off-putting how?" Tj asked as she turned onto the highway.

"She'd make statements that led people to believe she was a psychic of some sort. She claimed she didn't have any special powers; she just noticed things. She'd take one look at you and blurt out your deepest thoughts and secrets like they were tattooed across your forehead."

"So people thought she was a freak."

"Pretty much. She became friends with your grandma but never made other friends in the area. When she was seventeen, she met a man from Vengeance. They became friends and eventually married, which was when she left Serenity. According to what Nona shared with us, they had a daughter who died giving birth to Kiara. Nona ended up raising Kiara because her father wanted nothing to do with her. I'm not entirely sure what happened after that point."

"So you continued to see Nona after Grandma died?"

"She didn't come by to visit as she had when Grandma was alive, but I'd run into her from time to time, and we'd chat. Unlike many of the people in Vengeance, she never took to the isolation and continued to make trips into town. I actually hadn't seen her for quite a while until a year or so ago. She showed up at the senior center and asked to join us for bingo. I recognized her and offered to introduce her around. She seems to enjoy spending time with the group and has actually made several friends since she's been coming to play."

"Is that where she met Hazel?"

"No. Hazel knew her from before. She was, in fact, one of the kids who teased Nona as a teenager. Hazel once told me that she very much regrets the way she treated the newcomer to our area and has gone out of her way to be nice to her."

"Which is amazing, because Hazel is rarely nice to anyone." Tj laughed.

"Hazel is a decent woman. She's had a hard life. Harder than most realize. She tends to speak her mind, which makes her seem a lot gruffer than I believe she actually is."

"Yeah, I know you're right. She usually has a lecture of one type or another for me when I stop by the post office, but in my heart I know that if push came to shove, she'd be there for me."

"Did I mention Roy called looking for you earlier?" Ben asked.

"No, but I spoke to him. I was helping him interview Fenton Ridley about Tonya Overton's death. Boggs won't allow anything formal yet."

"Sounds like Boggs. Does Roy suspect something?"

"He has reason to believe Fenton and Tonya were having an affair when they first started working together."

"Doesn't seem like something Fenton is likely to share," Ben commented.

"He didn't. If you want my opinion, he's either innocent of the affair and the murder or a really confident liar. Not that I was able to ask him any direct questions, but he let me know he realized what I was doing. Roy is going to keep digging. If he can find anything significant, he can use it to get Boggs to allow them to pick up Fenton for a formal interrogation."

"Might need Dylan for that."

"Yeah, well, I guess they can cross that bridge when they get to it," Tj said.

"The café should be up ahead on the right," Ben said.

Tj slowed the vehicle as they approached a light in the distance. It was beginning to get dark, and the section of road they'd been traveling was narrow and unlit, so the lights from the coffee shop were clearly distinguishable.

"Yup. It looks like this is it."

She pulled into the parking lot. The coffee shop where Hazel had arranged for them to meet Nona was as dingy as it was small. Tj suspected the only reason it even existed was because of the single-pump gas island in the front, which provided the first fueling station since leaving the larger city at the base of the mountain.

Nona was waiting at a table in the corner. Ben had indicated that the woman was in her seventies, but to Tj, she looked a lot older. She had long white hair braided to her waist and wore a long skirt, a peasant top, and black work boots on her feet. Nona was hunched over the table, where she nursed a cup of some hot liquid. She reminded Tj of a fortune-teller she had seen at a carnival when she was a young girl.

There were only two other tables occupied when Ben and Tj arrived, one by a pair of truckers Tj suspected had arrived in the two eighteen-wheelers parked in the front, and the other by four young men who looked to be of high-school age. One of the boys wore a letterman's jacket from a high school at the foot of the mountain, so Tj imagined they were in town for the weekend.

"Thank you for meeting us," Ben began as he slid into the booth across from the woman. "This is my granddaughter, Tj," he added as she sat down beside him.

"You're the one looking for my Kiara?" Nona looked Tj

directly in the eye. She appeared to be studying her. Tj imagined that she was trying to decide whether to trust her.

"Yes, ma'am." Tj smiled. "Kiara came to the resort my family owns in order to participate in a beauty contest. She arrived on the bus with the others but never checked in. Have you heard from her in the past couple of days?"

The woman looked as if years of struggle had taken their toll. "I haven't spoken to Kiara since she ran away over a year ago. We were close once, but when things became tense, I'm afraid I wasn't there for her the way I should have been. I didn't even know she was coming to town."

"Can you tell us what happened?" Tj asked. "I realize it isn't any of our business, but if we can understand why she left, maybe we can figure out where she might be now."

Nona sat quietly. "Why do you seek my Kiara? Has she done something wrong?"

"No, she hasn't done anything wrong," Tj answered. "We just want to make sure she's okay. If she's changed her mind about the competition, we can take her name off the roster, but given the fact that she left rather abruptly, we feel it's our responsibility to ensure her welfare."

"I was surprised to hear she entered a beauty contest," Nona admitted.

"Frannie mentioned Kiara wanted to go to college," Tj offered. "I understand that part of the prize is a scholarship to the college of the winner's choice."

"That makes sense. Kiara wanted to go to college more than anything. She felt it was her calling to be a doctor."

"Is that why she left Vengeance?"

"No, not completely. I raised Kiara until two years ago. Her father thought I had been too lenient with the girl and decided to have her move back home with him. I fought his decision, but as her biological parent, it was his choice to do as he saw fit. After much consideration, Kiara's father decided to marry her to a boy in the community."

"So she ran away."

"She did," Nona confirmed. "I hate to admit it, but I did very little to stop her father from following through with his plan to unite the two. I realized that a union with Aaron would make Kiara's life easier. He's a nice young man who is well respected and popular in our community. I hoped that perhaps, as his wife, Kiara would finally gain acceptance among the group. I only wanted what was best for my granddaughter, but she didn't see it that way. When she left Vengeance, she left us all behind."

"Is this her fiancé?" Ben showed Nona the drawing.

"Yes, that is Aaron."

"He met Kiara at the bus," Tj informed Nona. "The two left together and she hasn't been seen since. Could he have hurt her?"

Nona considered this. "Aaron wouldn't hurt her. In spite of everything, I believe he loves her. It has been over a year since she left, but still he waits for her to return. Aaron is a popular young man in our settlement who could have his choice of a wife, but still he waits."

"Might they be together somewhere?" Ben tried. "Maybe Aaron managed to talk Kiara into running away with him."

"I saw Aaron this morning. He didn't mention anything, but perhaps I should have a chat with him, now that I know Kiara is missing."

"I would appreciate it if you'd call and let me know what you learn." Tj handed the elderly woman a napkin with her cell phone number written on it.

"I'll see what I can find out." Nona looked at Tj. She smiled, a tired and withered smile. "Thank you for caring. I'll be sure to contact you once I've spoken to Aaron. If he doesn't know of her whereabouts, I'd appreciate it if you'd keep looking. I doubt that anyone from the village other than Aaron will care one way or the other."

By the time Ben and Tj returned to the resort, Jenna was there talking to Doc, who had taken second place in the competition. The men went to the bar, while Jenna and Tj headed toward the fire pit Tj had reserved.

The beach was crowded as locals and visitors alike gathered to listen to the band. Tj hadn't eaten dinner, so she stopped by the house to gather the wine and cheese she'd promised, while Jenna went on ahead to start the fire. When Tj arrived at the beach, she saw that their friend, Kyle Donovan, had joined Jenna as well.

"Hey, Kyle. I thought you were on mom duty," Tj said.

Kyle's mother had decided to move to Serenity to be near her son and had been living with him while she looked for a townhouse to purchase. Tj had first met Kyle the previous October when he was brought to the resort by her old friend and Kyle's grandfather, Zachary Collins. Kyle never had the chance to meet Zachary, but the intense week that followed the man's murder had served to bond Tj and Kyle as best friends forever.

"I needed a break," blond-haired, blue-eyed Kyle admitted. "I love my mom, but living with her for the past month has put a strain on our relationship. I ran into Jenna earlier in the day and she mentioned the two of you were getting together, so I decided to join you. I hope that's okay."

"More than okay." Tj handed Kyle a glass. Luckily, she had brought several bottles of wine and extra glasses just in case she ran into anyone she knew. "I've missed you since your mom has been in town. Has she found a place?"

"Not yet. We've looked at several very nice condos, as well as a couple of small houses, but she seems to find a problem with each one. I told her to choose something she loves, that money is no object, but she still insists on looking for a good deal."

"She does know how much money you inherited, doesn't she?" Jenna asked as she poured everyone wine. Luckily for Tj, Jenna, her lifelong best friend, had accepted Kyle into their close-knit group as easily as she had.

"I've never given her an exact number. Heck, I don't even know the exact number. I've used words like tens of millions, though, and she's staying with me in the huge lakeside estate Zachary left me, so I think she gets the idea."

"Maybe she just likes living with her son," Tj pointed out. "Moving to a new town after twenty years in the same place would be hard for anyone. She doesn't know anyone here yet, so I'm sure she's lonely."

Kyle tossed another log on the fire before answering. Sparks danced in the air as the heat from the burning embers ignited the sap contained within the wood. "I guess that's true, but I'm not sure our relationship can survive a permanent arrangement. I love the idea of her being close by so she can be a regular part of my life, but I also need my own space. After my dad died, my mom began to focus all her attention on me. I get it; I'm all she has left. But at times her need to be involved in every part of my life can be intense, if you know what I mean. I feel like I'm past the point where I want to have someone who watches what I eat and worries if I'm out too late. How do you deal with living with your dad as an adult?" Kyle asked Tj.

She shrugged. "It's not too bad. My dad tends to keep to

himself. If I want his opinion about something, he's always happy to sit down and talk, but he doesn't meddle."

"My mom has started picking out my clothes," Kyle complained. "And she insists on doing the laundry. She caught me dumping a load in the washer without sorting or pretreating when she first moved in, and now she removes the clothes from my hamper before it's even full. I told her that I preferred to do my own laundry, but she insists that she wants to help out around the house since I'm letting her stay with me."

"I wouldn't mind someone doing my laundry," Jenna mused.

"She donated some of my clothes to the drive the church was having," Kyle pointed out. "She didn't even ask; she just went through my closet and pulled out everything she thought was past its prime. When I complained, she told me that I needed to present a certain image that didn't include my favorite sweatshirt with the frayed wrists or my jeans with the paint stains on them."

"Yikes." Jenna laughed.

"And don't even get me started on the diet she has me on."

"Diet?" Tj asked. Kyle had the most amazing body she had ever seen. Underwear models would envy him. "You certainly don't need to diet."

"It's not a weight-loss diet as much as a health-food diet. She went through my cupboards and threw out all my junk food. She read about the danger of eating too much white sugar, so now the only sweets I'm allowed in my own house are fruits."

"Oh, man, you have a problem," Tj sympathized. "A kitchen without chocolate is a kitchen without a heart."

"You should talk to your mom about getting involved at the senior center," Jenna suggested. "It would give her something to do and help her make friends."

"She's not exactly old," Kyle said.

"No, but Mom and Bonnie hang out there, and they aren't any older than your mother," Jenna pointed. "Although the facility is known as the senior center, they offer a wide range of options."

"Grandpa loves it," Tj added. "And your mom already knows a few of the regulars. They play bingo on Tuesdays and Thursdays. You should have her try it once to see if she likes it."

"I'm sure she can go with Mom and Bonnie," Jenna offered. "I'll have Mom invite her."

"Thanks; that would be nice."

Tj set the fruit, cheese, olives, freshly baked baguettes, crackers, and sliced deli meats she'd brought from the house on a blanket.

It was a perfect summer night. It was plenty warm by the fire, there were a million stars in the sky, and the band in the distance provided music while not being so close as to inhibit conversation.

Tj loved sitting on the beach with the moonlight shimmering on the lake as she unwound and relaxed with her friends. It was one of her favorite summertime activities.

"This is really good." Kyle popped one of the green olives stuffed with blue cheese she'd brought into his mouth.

"Yeah, what's with the fancy?" Jenna asked. "When you said wine and cheese, I figured canned cheddar on crackers would be the offering."

"I can cook," Tj argued.

"Did you actually cook?"

"No, but I assembled. I have five kinds of cheese, three kinds of olives, and marinated tomatoes with buffalo mozzarella, as well as a delightful selection of meats and spreads."

"I'm impressed." Jenna smiled.

"Well, don't be. I was lying about the assembling. The chef at the Grill put this together for me."

"We'll have to thank him; this is delicious," Kyle said.

"I guess you've heard about the dead Tropical Tan employee," Tj asked Kyle as he helped himself to a second serving of everything.

"I've heard tidbits through the local gossip hotline, but it doesn't seem like anyone knows much at this point, other than the fact that the woman was found floating in the lake."

"It just happened yesterday and the sheriff's office was keeping it quiet until the Tropical Tan staff had a chance to tell the models," Tj explained. "I'm sure by tomorrow the cat will be completely out of the bag."

"So do we know what happened?" Kyle wondered.

"I found Tonya tied to an anchor in Secret Cove. Actually, Echo found her; I just followed along. I talked to Roy earlier and he didn't seem to have any definitive leads, but he's looking into some chatter about an affair gone bad between Tonya and the head of the Tropical Tan Corporation, Fenton Ridley. Boggs isn't permitting Roy to formally interrogate Fenton, so I got him drunk and had a chat with him."

"You got him drunk?" Jenna's eyes widened.

"I tried to get him drunk. It didn't seem to work, even though he drank half a bottle of scotch. Anyway, the man claimed to be friends with Tonya but nothing more. I have to say, I believe him."

"What's going to happen next?" Kyle asked.

Tj shrugged. "I imagine we'll know more by tomorrow. Dylan was planning to go to Reno today to check out Tonya's movements after she arrived on the flight from Miami while he was picking up his sister and nephew."

"I wonder how that's going," Jenna said.

"I wish I knew." Tj sighed. "This is the first relationship I've had in which the outcome depends on the whim of a third party."

"Yeah, I guess it is sort of an odd situation," Kyle said. "Is Dylan still planning to move if his sister won't stay?"

"He says he is. Part of me thinks I should just move on. Dylan has indicated as much several times of late. He doesn't want me waiting around for him when he knows we might not have a future. Even if he can convince his sister to stay, I don't think there's going to be room in his life for a romance. The more I think about it, the more I realize Dylan might not be available for anything more than a friendship for a long time, if ever. And I do get it. I know Ashley and Gracie come first in my life, so I can understand how Justin comes first for Dylan."

"I guess I have to admire him for that," Kyle said.

"It might be easier if he was being a jerk."

"You haven't said what's going on with the missing model," Jenna said.

"Not a lot." Tj filled them in on her conversation with Nona, as well as her discussions with Hazel and Frannie.

"It does seem odd that the girl would just take off," Kyle said. "Especially if she knew her sister was here to meet her."

"We don't actually know that Kiara realized she was here. I suppose I should ask Annabeth about that if I see her again. Either way, after speaking to a few people about Kiara, it doesn't fit that she'd just take off with the guy she ran away from in the first place."

"Maybe she changed her mind about getting married," Jenna speculated. "If her fiancé met her at the bus, he might have had a plan to win her back."

"Seems unlikely," Tj said. "Besides, if she changed her

mind, why wouldn't she let anyone know that she was dropping out of the contest? The more I think about it, the more certain I am that something happened to her."

"Something like what happened to Tonya Overton?" Kyle asked.

CHAPTER 10

Friday, June 20

Tj got up early the next morning and went for a jog along the beach. Although it was early in the season, the marina was already filled with boats of different shapes and sizes. During the summer months, sailboat races were held during the sunset hour on Wednesday and Friday nights.

Families from both Serenity and Indulgence came to the beach to barbecue and watch the graceful boats with their beautiful sails compete for points that accumulated throughout the season, leading up to a grand finale over Labor Day weekend.

The resort was quiet since the only guests in residence slept in well past sunrise. Echo chased the geese that were combing the beach for scraps left from the previous day's picnickers. Most of the larger forest animals tended to stick to the woods, but every now and then Tj would come across a mama bear and her cubs out for a morning swim.

Tj settled into a comfortable rhythm as she thought about their conversation with Nona. She was anxious to find out what information she might have gained when she returned to the compound. Nona seemed certain that Aaron didn't have anything to do with Kiara's disappearance, but Tj wasn't so sure. She decided that if she hadn't heard from the woman by the end of the day, she'd have her grandpa try to get hold of her.

And if Kiara's disappearance wasn't enough to worry about, she was also getting pulled into Tonya Overton's murder investigation. Roy suggested an affair between Tonya Overton and Fenton Ridley had occurred, although Fenton hadn't said anything to indicate that he harbored ill will toward Tonya. But he had been in Serenity when the murder occurred, and he'd admitted to having dinners with the dead woman when they were home in Miami. He also indicated that he was close to all the employees he traveled with, and that his second wife wasn't at home a lot. It seemed reasonable that he might indulge in an extramarital fling when she was away.

Tj wound her way through the forest, taking advantage of the slight rise in perspective before circling back around to the beach for a final sprint to the large log structure she shared with the most important people in her life. She was just entering the house through the front door when her phone rang.

It was Dylan. Tj answered the phone and greeted him.

"Hey, Dylan," Tj greeted him.

"Tonya Overton rented a car shortly after she landed in Reno," Dylan said, jumping right in.

"Good morning to you too."

"Sorry." Tj could hear Dylan take a deep breath. "My sister decided to take a later flight, so she didn't come in yesterday as planned. I didn't find that out until after I was already at the airport, which actually worked out okay because it gave me more time to look into Tonya's movements from the time she got off the plane until she ended up under twenty feet of water in Secret Cove. If things go as planned, Allie and Justin are coming in this morning. I'm in a bit of a rush to go pick them up."

"I understand. So what did you find out?"

"According to the man who was working the car rental counter at the airport, Tonya was alone when she rented the car. When I informed the company that she was found dead several hours after leaving the airport, they accessed the GPS tracking system. The car was found in the marina parking lot in Serenity. Based on what I can put together, it looks like she rented a boat about three hours after she rented the car."

"It's only an hour from Reno to Serenity," Tj pointed out. "Do we have any idea where she was for the other two hours?"

"Unfortunately, the system doesn't have a memory, so we don't have any way of knowing where she stopped before heading to the marina. The man at the boat rental said she had two men with her. He didn't get a good look at their faces; they had on dark glasses and hooded sweatshirts, as well as jeans and heavy shoes. He said the men kept their distance and let Tonya take care of the paperwork and payment."

Tj tucked the phone under her chin so she could pour herself a glass of juice as she listened. Echo had already helped himself to the water in his dish and was napping on the cool surface of the kitchen floor. There was still a chill in the air, but Tj was willing to bet it was going to be hot by afternoon.

"The men must have taken her to the cove, hit her on the head, and dumped her. Do you think she went with them willingly?" Tj asked.

"The man I spoke to indicated that she did," Dylan replied. "She had plenty of opportunity to call attention to herself or even escape, but she didn't. I suppose it's possible the men she was with weren't responsible for her death, but at this point, I'd consider them prime suspects. If this was Chicago, I'd try to access traffic cams to see if I could determine where the vehicle might have come from, but as we both know, Serenity doesn't have any."

"How about the marina? It seems like they would have cameras that would allow them to keep an eye on the boats. Many of them are docked there for the season, and a good percentage sit unattended a large portion of the time."

"I already tried that. The cameras did pick up the threesome getting into the boat, but they only showed the men from the back. Other than having a general idea of height and weight, we didn't get a whole lot to go on."

"And the boat?" Tj wondered. "Did the men return it?"

"No. When the boat was late coming in, the marina sent out a team to look for it. They found it on the beach. We've been unable to find anyone who saw the men drop it there. And there are too many footprints in the area to be of any use. We're having the boat dusted for prints, but it was a rental, and not a well-maintained one at that. There are a lot of prints. It's going to take us a while to sort through them."

"Any blood on board?" Tj asked. She frowned as she remembered the large wound on Tonya's head.

"None that was evident to the eye. Again, we have a team going over the entire interior of the boat."

"And the anchor?"

"Is the one used to weigh Tonya down," Dylan verified.

Tj grimaced. The memory of Tonya floating above the anchor was not one she cared to revisit. "Connor said Kiara was heading toward the cove. Do you think she was there to meet Tonya?"

"Perhaps," Dylan said. "I think we need to find Kiara. If she's involved in Tonya's death, we need to find out what she knows, and if she isn't, she may have seen something."

"And if she's dead as well?"

"That would be important to know. I spoke to the CEO of the Tropical Tan Corporation yesterday. He said Tonya was on probation with the company. It seemed she disappeared when the tour stopped in Vegas."

Odd that Fenton hadn't mentioned that when she talked to him. She considered filling Dylan in on her conversations with both Roy and Fenton but decided he had enough on his mind with his sister's pending arrival.

"One of the girls told me Tonya had gotten in over her head and owed a lot of money to the wrong people. Maybe whoever she owed money to caught up with her."

"I suppose it's possible. I have Roy checking her financials and Tim checking her phone records. I need to get going. I don't want to be late picking up Allie and Justin. I'll try to call you later."

"Okay. I hope we get this wrapped up so you can enjoy their visit."

"You and me both."

After her conversation with Dylan, Tj showered and dressed. By the time she got over to the lodge, the models were beginning to emerge from their rooms. The day would be a busy one for the girls in the competition. The Tropical Tan Corporation had set up a series of photoshoots featuring the models in different attire at various locations around the lake.

"Morning, Tj," the model named Chloe called out to her.

"Good morning, Chloe. Care to join me?"

"I can't stay long. The group is about to leave, but I saw you sitting here and realized it was my chance to ask about Kiara. Any news?"

"I'm afraid not."

Chloe's face fell.

"Don't worry; we'll keep looking for her. Have you thought of anything else that might help us?"

"No," Chloe said. "It doesn't make sense that she would just take off. She wanted to win this thing. We talked about how the scholarship could change someone's life, and we both hoped it wouldn't be wasted on some girl who wouldn't even use it."

"I suppose that happens pretty often," Tj said.

"More often than not," Chloe said. "I'm afraid something has happened to her. And after what happened to Tonya..."

"Did you know Tonya well?" Tj asked.

Chloe shrugged. "I suppose. I mean, we didn't hang in the same social group, but she's been around for the whole competition, so we talked a few times."

"Did she ever mention a boyfriend?"

Chloe paused and thought over the question.

"I don't think so," Chloe answered. "I never saw her with a man, but I had the feeling there was someone she was getting over. She had a bit of a gambling problem, and it's my guess that her guy dumped her after the Vegas fiasco."

"Vegas fiasco?" Tj decided the best approach was to act as if she didn't know anything about Vegas and see what Chloe had to say.

"Tonya took off and went on a gambling spree. Mr. Ridley was furious. We all thought she'd get fired, but she didn't."

If Tonya had had an affair with Fenton Ridley, she could have used that fact as leverage to keep her job when she got in trouble while on assignment.

"Did Tonya ever mention any family?" Tj asked.

"She didn't talk about her life outside of her job at Tropical Tan to anyone. Ever. I got the feeling she was covering up a pretty rocky past. Sometimes the only way to start over is to walk away from where you've been."

"Yeah, I guess so."

"You know," Chloe added, "this may be nothing, but with both Kiara missing and Tonya dead, it could mean something."

"Go on," Tj encouraged.

"After the Vegas situation, it seemed like Tonya's relationship with Kiara changed. For the worse. In the beginning it seemed like they were friends, but then after Vegas I never saw them hang out together again. Kiara seemed really upset about Tonya's behavior, more so than normal if all they had was a passing relationship. Kiara was a lot more serious than the other girls, so it could be that she didn't approve of gambling, but if you ask me, there might have been more to it."

"You said Tonya and Kiara were friends. Would you say that prior to Vegas Tonya seemed closer to Kiara than to any of the others?"

"I don't know. Maybe. The initial rounds of the spokesmodel competition were held regionally, and Kiara and I weren't in the same region, so I didn't get to know her until just before Vegas. I suppose I might be reading more into the situation than is warranted. I should go," Chloe announced as the other models filed out of their rooms. "It looks like they're loading up the vans."

"Maybe we can talk later?" Tj suggested.

"I'd like that."

Tj liked Chloe. Unlike many of the other models who seemed so superficial, Chloe was genuinely nice. She seemed to care about Kiara, even though she'd only met her recently, and she was the only one who had shown any real emotion over Tonya Overton's death. Tj usually didn't pick a favorite in the contest, but this year she hoped Chloe would win.

* * *

When Tj returned to the house, Annabeth was sitting on the front stoop waiting for her.

She wore a blue dress just slightly less tattered than the yellow one she'd worn on Wednesday. She had on flip-flops that looked to be at least a size too small and, even though there was a slight chill in the air, she wasn't wearing any sort of sweater or cover-up.

"I'm glad you came by," Tj said to the girl. She sat down on the step next to her. "I was worried about you after you took off the other day."

"I'm sorry. I didn't want Aaron to see me. He would have told Papa."

"And you would have been in trouble for being here?"

"We aren't supposed to leave the settlement. I leave all the time and he never misses me, but if Aaron had seen me, he would have told on me for sure."

"The resort is a good fifteen miles from Vengeance. How did you get here?"

"I rode my bike."

Tj noticed an old bicycle propped up next to the house for the first time.

"Papa doesn't know I have it. Kiara gave it to me before she left so I could get into town if I needed to. I keep it in our secret spot so no one will find out that I have it."

"You rode that old bike fifteen miles?"

Annabeth shrugged. "It's not so bad."

"Fifteen miles is quite a trip on a bike without gears or a padded seat. You must be thirsty after such a long ride. Would you like to come inside for something to drink?"

"Yes, thank you."

"So what can I do for you, Annabeth?" Tj asked as she led the girl in through the house toward the kitchen.

"I wanted to ask if you found out anything about Kiara. I overheard Nona talking to Aaron. She said she was still missing. I'm afraid something bad happened to her."

Tj indicated that Annabeth should have a seat at the kitchen table while she poured lemonade into tall glasses filled with ice. "Did Kiara tell you she was coming to this area?"

"No. I haven't spoken to her since she left over a year ago." Annabeth gulped the juice down in one breath, so Tj refilled the glass and left the pitcher on the table.

"Then how did you know Kiara was going to be here on Wednesday?" Tj asked.

"Aaron told me," Annabeth answered.

"Did he mention how he knew Kiara was going to be here?" Tj sat down in a chair across from the girl.

"No, he didn't say."

"Did you know if Aaron planned to meet Kiara on Wednesday?" Tj asked.

Annabeth thought about it. "No. Things didn't end well between them. When Kiara left, he seemed mad, so I figured he wouldn't want to see her even if he knew she was coming."

Tj made a mental note to follow up on this seemingly minor detail. If they could find out how Aaron knew to meet the bus, they might be able to uncover who else could be involved in Kiara's disappearance. When she and her grandpa talked to Nona the day before, she'd indicated that she hadn't known Kiara was planning to be in the area. Could she have been lying?

"Are you and Nona close?" Tj asked.

"Yeah, pretty close," Annabeth answered. "She isn't my real grandma, but she watches out for me when my dad isn't around."

"When Nona was talking to Aaron, how did he seem?" Tj asked.

"Seem?" Annabeth finished her second glass of lemonade, so Tj refilled the glass.

"Was he surprised Kiara was missing? Did he act mad or scared?"

Annabeth thought about it. "He didn't seem mad or surprised. Do you think Aaron knows where Kiara is?"

"I don't know. Maybe. What about your dad? Did he seem angry, scared, or surprised when he heard Kiara was missing?"

"No. My dad doesn't care about anyone, especially Kiara. He says she's dead to him. I don't think he cares about her disappearance one way or the other."

Tj couldn't imagine writing off or disowning your own child, even if you were mad at them.

"Did Kiara have any friends?" Tj asked. "Maybe someone in the settlement or in town?"

Annabeth wound her long hair around her finger as she considered the question. She was a pretty girl, if somewhat unkempt. It was obvious she didn't have anyone in her life to teach her about proper hair or skin care. "Sometimes she'd mention someone named Lori. I think they met in the library."

"Do you remember a last name?"

"No. I don't think Kiara ever said."

Annabeth was eying the pitcher of lemonade, so Tj refilled her glass again. "Would you like something to eat?" she asked. "I have a fresh fruit salad and stuff to make sandwiches."

"Thank you. I am hungry."

Tj turned toward the refrigerator to retrieve the ingredients she'd need. "Tuna or egg salad?"

"Either is fine."

"I have both prepared, so feel free to choose one," Tj said.

"Tuna, then."

Tj retrieved the appropriate bowl, as well as a fruit salad her grandpa must have made containing watermelon, cantaloupe, strawberries, blackberries, and grapes. It really did look good, so Tj made a bowl for herself as well.

"Is this Kiara?" Tj heard Annabeth ask. Tj turned to see Annabeth looking at the head shot of Kiara that Leiani had given her the other day. She'd left it sitting on the counter.

"Yes. That's a photo she had taken for the competition."

"She looks so beautiful," Annabeth gasped. She touched her own stringy hair. "So different. When I first looked at it, I didn't even recognize her."

"The girls in the contest have their hair and makeup done by professionals before each photoshoot," Tj explained.

"I wish I could get my hair cut like that," Annabeth breathed.

"They don't have hairdressers in Vengeance?" Tj asked as she set a plate with a sandwich and fruit salad down in front of the young girl.

Annabeth giggled. "No. Most just wear their hair braided."

Tj remembered that Nona wore a long braid.

"Do any of the residents work in town?" Tj figured anyone with a job would need to adhere to proper grooming guidelines.

"No. Some of the people leave to get jobs, but then they don't continue to live in Vengeance."

"How do they pay for goods and services?"

"Most sell things or do odd jobs. My dad cuts and sells wood, and we have women who make quilts and other hand-sewn items. Quite a few families sell eggs, honey, and produce at the farmers markets during the summer. I know of one man who plows snow in the winter, and there are some, like Nona, who just have money. It's not expensive to live where we do.

There's no rent or utilities, and we grow most of our own food."

"It sounds nice."

Annabeth shrugged. "It can be, if you like that sort of thing. A lot of the kids who grow up there stay, but I want to go to school, like Kiara."

"You don't have a school?"

"There's a woman who gives classes at her house, but they're boring so I usually don't go. I like to read. Nona gets me books."

"What are your favorite kinds of books?" Tj asked.

"I like books about animals. And I like mysteries. I'm pretty sure I've read all the Nancy Drew books."

"Do you ever read books like the type they have in schools?"

"Nona got me some books about history, and I like math. I guess my favorites are books about science. Especially stuff about space. Nona tries to help me learn new things, but she can't help with stuff like algebra. When I get older, I'm going to learn everything I can about math and science. Kiara knows a lot of stuff. I keep hoping she'll decide to come home."

"Do you think she was planning to do that? Come home?"

Annabeth shrugged. "I don't know. She told me she would come for me when she got settled, but she never did."

"And your mom?"

"I don't have a mother," Annabeth informed her. "She went away when I was little."

"I'm so sorry. My mom left when I was young as well. I know how hard it is to grow up without a mom."

Annabeth shrugged. "It's okay. I had Kiara before she left. She didn't live with us when I was little, but she always took care of me. Now that she's gone I get lonely, but I have a lot of freedom because there's never anyone around to tell me what to do. Do you think you're going to be able to find Kiara?"

"I'm going to try," Tj promised.

"Can I help?"

Tj thought about it. "Actually, you can. I need you to go back to Vengeance and listen to what people are saying. Watch what they're doing. See if anyone seems interested in where Kiara might be. I'll do the same thing around town, and then we'll meet up to compare notes."

Annabeth smiled. "Like spies."

"Yeah. Like spies. But like a good spy, you have to be very careful not to let anyone know you're spying. Not even Aaron."

"What about Nona?" Annabeth asked.

"Not even Nona. You need to stay home and act like you normally do. Maybe we can meet tomorrow and talk about what we each find out."

"I can come out to the resort if you'll be here."

Tj hated to think about the girl riding her bike that far. "Maybe I can meet you somewhere and give you a ride."

"That's okay. I like to ride my bike, and I like to get away. Can I have some more fruit?"

"Certainly." Tj took her plate. "You must have been very hungry."

"Yeah. I guess it's been a while since I ate." Annabeth looked around while Tj refilled her plate. "I love your house. I bet it's nice to live here."

"It is nice."

"Do you live in this great big place all by yourself?"

"No." Tj set the plate of fruit down in front of the girl. "I live here with my grandfather, my dad, and my two sisters."

"And your dog." Annabeth reached down to pet Echo, who had been sitting at her feet the entire time she'd been there.

"And Echo, and four cats too."

"Cats? Can I see them?"

"Sure. We can go look for them after you eat. I'm betting they're sleeping on the beds upstairs."

"I've always wanted a kitten. I found one and brought it home one time, but Papa wouldn't let me keep it. He said we didn't need another mouth to feed. Kiara said I could get a kitten when I go live with her." Annabeth's eyes teared up. "Do you think she's okay?"

"I think she is," Tj said, trying to sound positive. "Don't worry." She hugged the girl. "We'll find her."

CHAPTER 11

Since the models were off-site, the resort was basically deserted except for the contestants from town who were setting up for the annual barbecue cook-off. The models were due to return by midafternoon and would most likely be found lounging by the pool, deepening the tans they all depended on. Spectators would begin arriving for the cook-off at about four, and the first band of the evening was set to start playing at around five. Which meant that Tj had a few—although very few—hours to herself to look into Kiara's disappearance, as she'd promised Annabeth she would.

Kyle had offered to come over and help out when she'd spoken to him the previous evening. Jenna was going to be tied up at the Antiquery until around four, but promised to come by when she was finished for the day.

Ben and his friends, Doc and Bookman, were entered in the barbecue cook-off, as they were every year. The men were already setting up, so Ben assured her he would be on-site should anything come up or need attending to while she was away.

Her best course of action was to meet Kyle in town. The town of Serenity was sponsoring a celebration of sorts in the park, and Frannie had mentioned she was going to set up the bookmobile near the bandstand for the day to take advantage of the increased number of potential customers for the new and used books she sold to help provide funding for the public library. As it did for every event and celebration, Serenity had gone all out to make its small-town appeal even more charming. The Town Council had granted the merchants a reduction on their business license fees if they agreed to participate in the campaign to beautify Main Street by hanging an ever-changing array of objects on the lampposts that lined it. During the summer months, huge baskets of flowers that draped several feet toward the ground were hung on both sides of the busy highway.

While the majority of the weekend events took place at the resort, the town took advantage of the extra tourists in the area by holding events of their own. When Tj and Kyle arrived, several locals were participating in a dog parade. Maybe Tj should have brought Echo. She'd been so busy of late that she hadn't been spending as much time with her canine buddy as she would have liked. While she had managed to take him out for at least a short walk every day, it had been ages since they'd enjoyed a day-long hike through the deserted forest together.

The schedule taped to a sandwich board announced that following the parade there would be a pie-eating competition, followed by lawn bowling. Tj didn't understand the appeal of eating an entire pie with one's hands tied behind one's back. The one and only time she'd tried it, she'd ended up with stains on one of her favorite pairs of pants and a blueberry up her nose.

As predicted, Tj found Kyle chatting with Frannie near the bandstand where she'd set up her bookmobile, an ancient van someone had donated to the county. Frannie had painted the exterior with bright colors and had the interior outfitted to store portable bookshelves that could be taken out and set up for displays during special events. Most of the books were used ones the residents of Serenity had donated, but Frannie used the proceeds from the sale to buy a new selection of bestsellers.

"Tj, how are you, dear? I didn't expect to see you in town all weekend with everything you have going on at the resort."

"The models are off-site for a photoshoot," Tj explained.

"Ah. I imagine this must be the calm before the storm. Can I interest you in a book?"

Tj picked up a book to read the back cover. "The main reason we're here," she began, "is because we're still looking into Kiara Boswell's disappearance. Her sister Annabeth mentioned that Kiara spoke of a girl named Lori who she'd met at the library. Annabeth didn't have a last name, but I was hoping you'd know who Kiara referred to."

"She must mean Lori Sullivan. Lori and Kiara were both frequent patrons of the library before they left the area. I wouldn't say they were great friends, but they did chat from time to time. I remember one summer afternoon when the three of us were trapped in the library during an afternoon thunderstorm. The electricity went out and it was much too dangerous to venture outdoors, so we spent a couple of hours chatting."

"I know Lori," Tj said. "She graduated two years ago. I heard she went to Princeton."

"She did," Frannie confirmed. "I ran into her the other day. She's home for the summer."

"Do you happen to have a phone number for her?" Tj asked.

Frannie shook her head. "I don't have her cell number, but I might have her parents' home number in my records at the library. I can check when I'm done here."

"Thanks, but the number is probably listed. If I can't track it down, I'll let you know."

"I hope Kiara is okay." Frannie looked worried. "It's been

two days. You would think she would have checked in with someone if she had just changed her mind about the competition."

"Yeah, I'm worried about her too," Tj said. "Annabeth came by the resort this morning. She seemed certain Kiara would have contacted her by now if she was able to do so."

"I have to say I agree." Frannie frowned. "I didn't know Kiara well, but I do know she adored her half-sister."

"Did you get the idea that Annabeth is being neglected or abused?" Tj asked.

Frannie paused. She tended to be deliberate in her words and actions. "Kiara never said anything along those lines, specifically," Frannie said. "But I got the impression Kiara believed Annabeth was too bright a girl not to be attending school. Kiara often mentioned that education wasn't important in her dad's eyes, and if not for Nona, she would never have learned to read. Kiara shared that many of the females in the village never received any type of formal education. She also mentioned Annabeth lacked supervision and was left to her own devices much too often. Have you talked to Nona?"

"Yeah, but she didn't even know Kiara was going to be in town. She made it sound as if she and Kiara had some kind of disagreement before she left Vengeance. If you think of anything else or hear anything, call me. You have my cell number."

"I do have your cell and I will call," Frannie promised. "And if you find out anything, please let me know."

"I'll do that."

Tj called information to get Lori's parents' number while Kyle returned to his vehicle to store the books he had bought. After a brief discussion, it was decided that Tj would ride with Kyle while they went to visit Lori, who was home and happy to speak to them, and then come back for Tj's vehicle when they were done. They stopped by the Antiquery first to pick up a pastry to offer Lori out of appreciation for her taking time out of her day to speak to them.

Jenna had several delicious-looking specials that day. Tj couldn't help but try a taste of the mini éclairs, which featured the best-tasting chocolate glaze she had ever eaten, while Kyle opted for a slice of rich and creamy Kahlúa pie.

The restaurant was packed, so Kyle and Tj sat at the counter in the kitchen, chatting with Jenna while she prepared plate after plate of sandwiches, burgers, salads, and specialty dishes.

Tj reached for a second helping of éclairs. Luckily, it looked like Jenna had plenty. "If I keep eating these, I'm going to get fat."

"Speaking of fat, I've been meaning to talk to you about something," Jenna responded.

Tj's face fell. "You think I'm fat?"

Jenna laughed. "No, I don't think you're fat. With all the exercise you get, you can't have more than two percent body fat."

"So what did you want to ask me about?" Tj pushed the napkin with the three éclairs she'd just helped herself to toward Kyle.

"I think I'm gaining weight, and I know I'm out of shape. I've felt tired and unenergetic lately, and the waistband on my jeans is getting tight. I heard there's a new dance aerobics class at the community center on Tuesday and Thursday nights. I thought I'd give it a try if you'll do it with me." Jenna rang the bell for her waitress to pick up an order.

"I thought you said I wasn't fat."

"You aren't, but I need this, and I know if I don't have someone to do it with, I'll sign up, pay my fee, maybe attend the first class, decide I'm too busy, and never go back. If you do it with me, you can bully me into attending every week."

Tj laughed. "You know that bullying people into working out is what I do for a living?"

"I know. So will you do it? Please?"

"If you want me to do it, I'm happy to, but you aren't getting fat. You look great," Tj insisted.

"Yeah, you look great," Kyle added. "It doesn't look like you've gained any weight at all."

"Tell that to my jeans that don't want to button any longer." Jenna groaned.

"Are you sure there isn't another reason your jeans are getting tight?" Tj asked. She knew Jenna and Dennis had been trying to have another baby. There had been one false call when Jenna thought she might actually be pregnant, but it turned out she'd been wrong.

"No." Jenna sighed. "No reason at all."

"Okay, let's do the class," Tj agreed "Who's teaching it?"

"I'm not sure. When I spoke to Harriet, she said she had someone in mind, but she didn't say who."

Harriet Kramer was the town secretary and responsible for booking activities in the community center, among other things.

"I'm sure it will be awesome." Tj turned to Kyle. "Want to join us?"

"Thanks, but tights and leotards don't do a thing for me."

"Oh, come on," Tj teased. "I bet you'd look adorable in tights. We could get matching leggings."

Kyle threw a mini cream puff at her.

Tj plucked it out of her hair and ate it. Jenna really was the best cook.

* * *

After Tj and Jenna had finalized their plans to sign up for the class, the discussion turned to which type of treat to bring as a gift for Lori and her parents. They decided to go with an assortment of freshly baked cookies, because Tj didn't know Lori well enough to judge her food preferences. Lori's parents owned a nice two-story house on the corner of Oak and Spruce. The area, known as the tree streets, was more of a residential neighborhood than was found in the rural parts of Paradise Lake. The houses were situated on small lots with lawns in the front yards and canals that provided boat lovers with direct access to the lake in the back. Personally, Tj wouldn't want to live where you could almost reach out and touch your next-door neighbor's house, but those who lived in the upper-middle-class neighborhood seemed to love it.

Lori blushed and smoothed a hand over her hair as she greeted Tj, who introduced her to Kyle. He really was a good-looking man: supermodel gorgeous, with shaggy blond hair, intense blue eyes, and a killer smile that had a tendency to melt hearts. Most of the women in town, whether married or single, young or old, had crushes on the community's newest millionaire.

"How have you been doing in college?" Tj asked as Lori led them through the house to an outdoor deck that featured a sitting area positioned near a delightful fountain.

"Really well," Lori answered. "I aced all of my classes last year, which I absolutely needed to do to get into medical school, which is amazing since I flunked high school biology."

"You flunked biology?" Tj asked. Lori had always been a serious student as far as she could remember.

"Warren Livingston was my lab partner."

"Ah." Warren was a year ahead of Lori and the school heartthrob. Tj wasn't surprised that Lori had trouble concentrating with such a distraction. "High school biology aside, I'm sure you'll have no problem getting into a good med school. You always did so well in school."

"Yeah, well, high school and college really aren't the same beast." Lori laughed.

"True."

"I appreciate you bringing the cookies," she said, sliding them onto a plate and setting it on the table. "Can I get you something to drink?" she asked. "Ice tea? Lemonade?"

Lori had been prepared with glasses and pitchers of both beverages on a counter that was part of an outdoor kitchen built into the covered patio behind the table where they sat.

"Lemonade would be nice," Tj answered.

"I'll have the same," Kyle added.

Lori poured the drinks and took a seat across from them. "So you're looking for Kiara Boswell?"

Tj had explained the reason for their visit when she'd called, but she hadn't gone into any detail on the phone.

"I don't know if she told you, but she entered the Tropical Tan spokesmodel competition," Tj began. "She arrived on the bus with the other girls, but then left with a man we believe to be her ex-fiancé, Aaron. No one has seen her since."

"I knew Kiara had entered the competition," Lori said. "She wasn't thrilled about the idea, but like me, she wants to be a doctor, so I figured the scholarship must have been more than she could resist. I know she didn't have the financial means to pursue her dream, so it made sense to me that when she found out about the scholarship included in the prize package, she signed up. But even though everything she told me made perfect sense, I got the feeling there was something more going on."

"Something more?" Tj asked.

"She didn't say so, but she seemed," Lori searched for the right word, "hesitant. She not only didn't seem very excited about the whole thing, but she almost seemed scared."

"Scared how?" Kyle asked.

"I don't know. It was more the tone of her voice. If I had to guess, she was nervous about something."

"Kiara was last seen with Aaron. Do you think she was afraid of him?" Tj asked.

"Aaron? No. She never said she was afraid of him. In fact, she really seemed to like him. She told me that he was as much a victim in the whole engagement fiasco as she was. She said he was a nice guy who would make someone a good husband, but she wasn't interested in marrying anyone, and especially not anyone from the village. I know she was concerned about hurting him when she left, but in the end she did what she needed to do."

"Annabeth indicated that Kiara planned to come back for her when she had a chance."

"Yes, she was concerned about her half-sister. She hated to leave her but had no way to provide for her. The sisters didn't grow up in the same household, but they were very close."

"Did Kiara ever tell you she was afraid of her father?" Tj asked.

Lori shyly glanced at Kyle as she considered the question. "I don't know if she was afraid of him. I do know she didn't really like him. She said he was a cruel and selfish man who blamed her for her mother's death and blamed Annabeth for her mother's desertion. Kiara was raised by her grandmother until the last couple of years. Annabeth lived with her father, but Kiara mentioned on more than one occasion that she was an independent soul who would do okay in life if she could get away from the isolation of the compound. Kiara wanted Annabeth to go to school. She wanted her to have options in life other than what the settlement offered."

"Do you think Kiara's father could have hurt her?"

Lori looked shocked by the question. "God, I hope not. Do you think that's what happened?"

"I don't know," Tj admitted. "Maybe. She did run away, and it seems like he's a less than kind man. From what I've learned, I can imagine him being someone who would take out his anger on a daughter who didn't obey him."

"I hate to think that's the case." Lori frowned. "She was—I mean is—such a sweet thing. I know her dad was upset when she left, but he is her father. I can't imagine he would hurt her."

Tj sighed. "Can you think of anyone else who might have wanted to hurt Kiara?"

"No." Lori shook her head. "I know that doesn't help you, but I can't imagine anyone wanting to hurt Kiara."

Tj finished her beverage. She glanced at Kyle, and then motioned that they should prepare to leave.

"If you hear from Kiara, will you please call us?" Tj asked.

"Sure, no problem. It was nice meeting you," Lori said, turning toward Kyle.

"It was nice meeting you too." Kyle shook her hand, and Lori looked like she might pass out. "And good luck with your studies. I'm betting you'll make a fantastic doctor."

"Thank you." Lori blushed.

"So what do you think?" Kyle asked as the pair walked down the rose-lined sidewalk back to the car.

"I don't know what to think," Tj said. "It seems like all roads lead back to the father and ex-fiancé, yet no one we've talked to feels either of them could have hurt Kiara."

"Do you think there's a possibility that she isn't hurt?" Kyle asked. "Perhaps she simply decided the contest wasn't for her and took off."

Tj thought about Kyle's question. "I would entertain that idea if it weren't for Annabeth. I find it hard to believe Kiara would take off without contacting her sister. Annabeth is worried about her. Wouldn't Kiara realize that and get in touch with her in some way if she were able to?"

"Do you think she's dead?" Kyle asked.

"God, I hope not."

CHAPTER 12

"It looks like the Playboy Mansion around here," Roy said as he walked with Tj. Many of the twenty-four models on-site were lounging by the pool while working on their tans.

"The girls are sunning themselves after a long day of modeling," Tj answered. "The pool policy is that proper bathing attire needs be worn at all times, but I have to say that some of these girls are liberally interpreting the definition of proper bathing attire."

Tj sat down on a picnic bench in the shade at the edge of the lawn where it bordered the sand. She invited Roy to join her. It was much less crowded here than it was either at the pool or on the sand, yet the view was still spectacular.

"So do you have news?" Tj wondered.

"A friend of mine who is an intern at the hospital thinks Tonya's head wound could have been due to a fall."

"A fall? So she wasn't murdered?"

"I'm not saying that exactly. She was tied to an anchor and dumped into the lake, but at this point, if my friend is correct, the source of the head wound should be relooked at. I'm trying to get Boggs to allow us to take a second look."

If Tonya died as a result of a fall, that could change things quite a bit. "What have you found out about Fenton?"

"Fenton Ridley first founded the Tropical Tan Corporation

more than twenty years ago. He used the money that his first wife inherited from her grandmother to get started. Once he started to make money, he began sleeping with anything in a bikini. His wife filed for divorce when their son was two."

Tj frowned. "Fenton made it sound like his wife left him due to his traveling."

"That doesn't line up with what was documented in the divorce papers," Roy said.

Tj thought back to her conversation with Fenton. He'd never actually said that his traveling was the reason for the divorce, though he'd insinuated it when he'd said he was a terrible husband and father.

"Okay, go on," Tj said.

"The divorce was beyond nasty. Ridley's wife insisted she should get a share of the current and future earnings from the company because it was her inheritance that allowed him to start it in the first place. Ridley argued that Tropical Tan was young and not worth much since all of the profits were being funneled back into the start-up. In the end, Ridley's wife got back the money she'd invested plus a small amount of interest. Ridley paid child support but wasn't an involved parent."

It seemed odd to Tj that his son would be on this trip with him if he hadn't shared a relationship with his father when he was a child.

"And the son?" Tj asked.

"Porter Ridley barely knew his father until he turned eighteen. That's when he sought out the father he hadn't seen since he was a baby. It appears Fenton convinced the boy that it was his mother who wouldn't allow the relationship he very much wanted. He gave his son a cushy job with a huge paycheck and the two have been close ever since, although it appears Porter has cut his mother out of his life."

"It doesn't make sense that Porter's mother could forbid his father from seeing him unless Fenton had done something truly heinous. Fenton has to have been lying."

"The only thing I can come up with is that Fenton's ex had something damaging to hold over his head. Either that or he didn't care about seeing his son or being a part of his life and didn't fight for the right to do so."

Tj looked out across the lake. The water was filled with kids swimming and splashing as they cooled off from the heat of the afternoon. Sounds of laughter filled the air. Tj couldn't imagine walking away from your own child.

"Okay, so Fenton cheats on his wife and abandons his child. Sixteen years later, his company is worth millions and his wife is out in the cold while he's reunited with his son. He ended up with the kid and the money. I know who the prime suspect would be if Fenton ends up dead."

"Tell me about it," Roy agreed. "Although the ex-wife remarried and is far from being out in the cold. I wouldn't feel too sorry for her."

"Okay, so back to the affair," Tj said. "Did you find out anything more about that?"

"There is no conclusive evidence that an affair occurred. We have the testimony of Tonya's ex-roommate, but that won't be enough, especially since she seems to be a bit of a flake. Fenton admitted to being friends and even going to dinner with Tonya while they were in Miami. I doubt Boggs will buy the fact that a sexual relationship existed without something more, and even if we could, it wouldn't mean he murdered her."

"And the new wife?"

"She's from money herself. This is her first marriage but certainly not her first affair; in fact, there's reason to believe a lack of fidelity goes both ways between Fenton and his wife. I'd like to have a conversation with her to see how she reacts to allegations of Fenton's infidelity, but Boggs is still forbidding it."

"It looks like we don't have a whole lot more than we did when we started."

"I'm not sure how we're going to prove anything if Boggs won't let us talk to the suspects," Roy said. "We don't have a lot to go on other than the men who were with Ms. Overton when she rented the boat. Unfortunately, we haven't been able to find anyone who can identify them."

"Someone has to have seen something. The marina is a busy place at this time of year. Maybe there are other boaters who were coming and going at the time Tonya was at the marina."

Roy started to answer but then stopped. He nodded toward something behind Tj's back.

She turned around. "Amber?"

"Sorry to interrupt, Miss Tj, but I wanted to ask about the extra cabin."

"What extra cabin?" Tj asked.

"The cabin that Mr. Ridley was supposed to use, ma'am. He told Leiani that he wouldn't be needin' it since he had a room in town, but young Mr. Ridley is at the desk askin' about it. Leiani left for the day, and I didn't feel comfortable makin' the decision on my own."

"Fenton Ridley's son is here?" Tj clarified.

"Yes, ma'am. He said he wants to use the cabin to entertain." Amber blushed. "He has a woman with him," she whispered.

"I see. Well, the cabin is paid for, so I don't see a problem with letting Mr. Ridley's son use it, but perhaps we should call Mr. Ridley and clear it with him first."

"You want me to call Mr. Ridley?"

Amber had a look of panic on her face.

"No, I'll do it in a few minutes. Let Mr. Ridley's son know that I'll be right over to see to things."

"Yes, ma'am."

"Sounds like the son is following in the father's footsteps." Roy chuckled.

"Yeah, seems like. If you want to wait, this should only take a few minutes."

"I should get back. I think we've covered everything. I'll call you later."

Tj came into the lodge through the back door. She was just about to make an appearance at the counter, where Fenton's son was waiting, when she saw Jazzy walk in through the front.

"What are you doing here?" Jazzy asked Porter.

"I work for Tropical Tan. This is the final week of the spokesmodel competition. Where else would I be?"

"But what are you doing here? After that fiasco with Tonya, I thought your daddy told you he didn't want you hanging around the models anymore."

Tj paused behind the doorjamb so she could hear what Jazzy and Porter were saying without them seeing her.

"Tonya was a jealous witch who decided to make my life hell after I tossed her aside. Besides, the harpy is dead. I doubt she's going to be able to tell my old man anything."

Silence.

"Did you kill her?" Jazzy asked.

"Of course I didn't kill her," Porter defended himself. "But I'm not going to pretend I'm sad that someone else did. The woman was a pain in my backside and we both know it."

"All she did was tell your dad that you'd been sleeping your way through the model pool, making promises that weren't yours to keep," Jazzy pointed out.

"These girls know the score."

"Maybe some of them do, but others..."

"You going to snitch to my dad about my being here?"

"I don't know. What's it worth to you for me to keep quiet?"

"What do you want?"

"You here alone?"

"No, I'm here with Haley," Porter informed Jazzy. "She went over to the bar to try to get us some drinks while I wait for that control freak of a resort manager to come and let me into a cabin."

Control freak?

"Haley is a baby," Jazzy responded. "Leave the poor thing be."

"A man has needs."

"You are such a jerk," Jazzy spat.

Tj carefully peeked around the corner. Jazzy had sauntered up to Porter and was rubbing her barely clad body against his fully clothed frame.

"Fortunately, I'm into jerks," Jazzy drawled. She ran a long acrylic nail down his chest. "Forget about Haley and let me take care of you."

Jazzy stood on tiptoe and kissed Porter on the mouth.

Tj thought she might gag as Porter grabbed Jazzy in one of the very few areas covered by her bikini. "Seems like being with you would be like watching a rerun. Maybe I'm looking for something new."

Jazzy whispered something in Porter's ear after tugging on his earlobe with her teeth. He smiled and slapped her on her rear.

"Okay, darling. I'm game, but we still need the cabin."

"No we don't." Jazzy took Porter's hand and led him up the stairs, no doubt to her room.

Tj felt her stomach churn as the couple walked away. There were some women in the world she would never understand. Porter was dripping with sleaze and still the woman wanted to sleep with him. It made no sense to her.

"Hey, Roy," she said after she'd dialed his cell and waited for him to answer. "I may have another lead for you to follow up on. It seems Fenton's kid has been sleeping with Fenton's mistress."

CHAPTER 13

The barbecue cook-off was one of Tj's favorite events of the long weekend, partly because she loved to eat, but also because of the friendly rivalry that had built up between the members of the community who participated each year. Traditionally, her grandpa and Jake Hanson both entered beef ribs, but this year Hunter had mentioned that he'd insisted his grandfather enter heart-healthy chicken instead. Doc would barbecue up his famous brisket, while retired county deputy Nolan Rivers favored pork ribs. Jake had recruited Hunter to be on his team, while Doc had arranged for Bookman's help and Kyle had agreed to assist Ben. The competition tended to attract the male residents in the area, so Tj and Jenna were left to their own devices while the men prepared their entries.

"I can't believe how good it smells out here." Tj took an appreciative breath of the smoke-filled air. The contestants had been preparing for hours and the aroma that permeated the area was more than enough to make her mouth water. Echo, who was standing next to her, was staring intently at the meat her grandfather was methodically turning to ensure an even distribution of heat and sauce.

"I can almost taste the smoke," Jenna agreed.

"One of the reasons I love summer so much is the smell of the wood smoke and family barbecues in the campground," Tj said. "There's nothing quite like waking up to the smell of bacon frying in a cast-iron skillet."

"You think I'd be immune to the smell of food cooking after working in a restaurant for the past eight years, but there's something about barbecue smoke that can't be beat. What time is the judging?" Jenna asked. Tradition dictated that the judges taste each entry before the contestants opened tasting to the general populace.

"Four. The guys should be ready for tasting by the public by five or so. Grandpa has been working on his secret sauce for weeks. I'm sure he's made at least five different batches, attempting to get the perfect combination of flavors. He swears these are going to be his best ribs yet."

"Not to play favorites, but my mouth has been watering for Doc's brisket since last year," Jenna commented. "I'm not sure what he puts into his rub to give it such a unique flavor, but it is to die for. I keep hoping he'll share the recipe."

"Good luck getting him to tell you." Tj laughed. Doc protected his recipe better than the feds protected the gold in Fort Knox. "I should wander down to the beach and make sure everything is set up for the band. Want to come along?"

Jenna shrugged. "Yeah, sure. Who's playing this year?" she asked as she set off with Tj, Echo trailing behind them.

"The Mud Stompers, followed by the Gator Gutters." Tj dodged a pair of boys who were chasing each other through the crowd with water guns. She momentarily considered asking them to take their game down to the beach, but they weren't hurting anything, and Tj could remember playing similar games when she was a kid.

"So hillbilly country?" Jenna guessed.

"Pretty much. The Mud Stompers mix it up a bit, but the crowd almost revolted last year when I tried to mix in some classic rock. Guess twangy country is the music of choice for the barbecue crowd. I do have a new band closing out the set. They're from the Bay area and play a blend of classic and modern rock. Since they come on last, the barbecue crowd will be gone and only the hardcore drinking crowd will be left."

"Ending the evening with some classic rock will be nice, although I'm always up for a little square dancing."

Tj laughed. "Remember when we had to spend two whole months square dancing in high school as part of our physical education rotation? The guys hated it."

"Yeah. I remember how happy Dennis was when he broke his leg a week into the semester. Everyone already had partners, so I had to dance with Ms. Brubaker until Toby Calvin moved and I was paired with Stella Long. It seemed like you had a lot more fun dancing with Hunter."

Tj looked out across the beach, which was crowded with bright umbrellas and families spread out on large blankets. This might turn out to be their best crowd yet. Tj turned to answer Jenna. "I had fun, but Hunter wasn't a fan. He kept kidding about asking his grandpa to put a cast on his leg even though he was fine."

Jenna laughed. "I remember that. Looking back, maybe he should have followed through with his threat, and then we could have been partners and really had fun."

"Seriously. I don't know why the guys fought it so much. Hunter was good. I'll have to coax him into the mix if people start dancing tonight. Too bad Dennis isn't here. Seems he owes you a few do-si-dos and promenades."

"He'd never do it in a million years."

Tj climbed up to the bandstand to make sure that everything that could be set up ahead of time had been, while Echo found a place in the shade to wait. The band would bring their own equipment and musical instruments, but speakers and microphones were provided by the resort to be used by all of the bands that played over the weekend.

"Speaking of Dennis, have you heard from him and the girls?"

"They're having a fabulous time camping and fishing." Jenna followed Tj up the wooden steps. "Kari caught her first fish yesterday. Part of me is sorry I missed it, but most of me is glad I'm here and not up at mosquito lake. The last time I went camping with Dennis and the girls, I had so many mosquito bites, you could barely see the skin in between."

"The little buggers do seem to like you," Tj said as she moved a microphone into place. The bandstand had been set up so that the backs of the musicians were to the lake and the crowd faced the awesome view. It really was magical when the sun set over the distant mountain and the fires in the pits strategically placed around the area were lit to provide warmth for the crowd.

Jenna helped Tj shove one of the larger speakers to the side, where it would be best utilized. "Dennis never gets bit and it looks like both girls are taking after him. I guess I'm the only one in the family who is cursed with sweet-tasting blood."

"It must be because of all the cookies you taste when you're coming up with new recipes," Tj suggested.

Jenna laughed. "You may have a point. How are Ashley and Gracie liking Disney World?"

Tj smiled at the memory of the conversation she'd had with them earlier in the day. "They're having so much fun. Apparently, Ashley loves the thrill rides and Gracie likes anything that spins. Rosalie plans to take the girls to several of the parks, including Epcot. Dad joins them when he's able to get away from the conference. They're even talking about extending the trip another few days so they can go over to the coast. I should have made more of an effort to go with them. It was kind of a last-minute thing, and I was afraid my dad would worry if I wasn't here to oversee things this weekend, but the truth of the matter is that I've hardly done anything. Julie and Leiani have done a good job of handling whatever's come up."

"Given that you have a dead Tropical Tan employee and a missing model, it's probably a good thing you were here," Jenna pointed out.

"Yeah, I guess that's true."

"Any news on either?"

"Actually, yes. It looks like not only was Fenton Ridley having an affair with Tonya, but his son might have been as well."

"You mean Tonya slept with the father and the son?"

"It's a strong possibility. Fenton isn't saying anything, but based on what I witnessed today, I totally believe Porter could be guilty of the deed."

"Why? What did Porter do?" Jenna asked.

Tj filled her in on the disturbing encounter she'd witnessed between Jazzy and Porter.

"Wow. As gross as I find the whole thing, I guess sleeping with your dad's mistress and having your dad find out and exile you from the other models could be a motive for murder."

"That's what I thought," Tj agreed. "Although, in all fairness, I don't actually know that Fenton found out about Porter and Tonya. And besides, there's more. There's a possibility that neither man murdered Tonya. In fact, it's possible she wasn't murdered at all."

"Okay, now I'm confused."

"Roy seems to think it's possible that the blow to Tonya's head could have been due to a fall."

"A fall? I thought the autopsy indicated a blow to the head by a rock."

"That's what the report says, but we both know that our local coroner is getting on in years. I'm going to ask Doc to take a look at the body and the original autopsy report. I should have done that in the first place, but given the fact that Tonya was also tied to an anchor, it seemed evident that she was murdered. And based on my own observation, a blow to the head fit. Do you think this speaker should be farther to the left?"

Jenna stood back. "No, I think it's good."

"Then I guess we're done here." Tj jumped off the bandstand and called Echo to her side. "Let's head over to the cabins and check to see whether the Tropical Tan folks need anything. They've been a fairly demanding group this year."

"Aren't they demanding every year?"

"Yeah, but this group seems particularly bad. If they run low on anything, you can be certain that someone is going to have a rant. They should change the title of the competition to Ms. Tropical Diva."

Jenna laughed. "Just two more days and the nightmare will be over. Besides, you have a missing girl to find and a suspicious murder to solve. That should be enough to keep you distracted."

"More than enough," Tj agreed as she stopped in the laundry to fill a cart with clean towels. It had been Leiani's idea to hold the Tropical Tan competition at the resort in the first place. And while it did bring in early revenue, which was important to ensure that each season got off to a good start, Tj found that she was having less and less patience with the finicky models.

"So why does Roy suspect a fall?" Jenna asked as she, like Echo, followed Tj across the resort after she'd gathered the supplies she'd anticipated she might need.

"A friend of his is an intern, and she noticed some anomalies."

"Have you asked Hunter about it?" Jenna wondered as she helped Tj drop off towels in one of the cabins the models had been using for massages. The furniture had been moved and the room partitioned so that multiple massage tables could be set up and still offer some privacy.

"Not yet, but I intend to. I figure I'll wait until after the barbecue judging and then talk to both Hunter and Doc. If nothing else, maybe I can have them both take a closer look at the report."

"Not to be dense or ask a stupid question, but does it really matter?" Jenna asked as they made their way to the next cabin. "We know Tonya is dead. We know someone tied an anchor to her ankle and sank her in Secret Cove. It seems like murder any way you slice it."

"When I asked Hunter about the medical examiner's report, he told me Tonya was dead when she went into the water. That would be pretty evident due to a lack of water in the lungs. I don't think even our coroner could mess that up. But what if Tonya slipped and hit her head and died as a result? Whoever she was with might have panicked and sunk the body. If that's what happened, then the person who did it would only be guilty of covering up a death, not murder."

Tj stopped in front of the cabin that was being used as a hair salon. The women lined up in chairs receiving blow-dries made her think of Annabeth and her desire to have her hair done. Maybe she could arrange something the next time she saw her. Nothing drastic, but perhaps a good wash and a trim.

"I'm still confused." Jenna stopped walking as Tj made the decision to go inside. "Are you investigating Tonya's murder or Kiara's disappearance?"

"Both. No, actually, neither," Tj corrected herself. "I don't know. I just know something went down, and I want to know what. Kiara is missing and may still be alive and in need of our help, so I guess finding her is my priority, but I have to admit to being curious about what happened to Tonya. Roy seems to be in over his head and there' more going on behind the scenes at the Tropical Tan Corporation than meets the eye."

Tj was finishing filling Jenna in on what she had learned from Roy when Chloe walked up.

"Afternoon, Tj," Chloe said.

"How was your day?" Tj asked the young girl, who was leaving the salon.

"Excellent. And yours?"

"It was pretty excellent as well. This is my friend Jenna. Jenna, Chloe."

"Happy to meet you," Jenna answered.

"Chloe is hoping to win the competition in order to gain the scholarship that's part of the prize package," Tj explained.

"That's fantastic. Where do you want to go to school?" Jenna asked.

"I haven't thought about it. I haven't had the financial resources to apply to top schools. I know there are a lot of good options out there, and I should look at everything each school has to offer. I guess I'll figure all that out if I can work out the rest."

"Makes sense. Good luck with tomorrow's events."

"Thank you. I have to admit I'm getting nervous," Chloe shared. "Tomorrow is the talent competition, and I plan to sing a song. I've never sung in front of a big crowd before. I'm afraid it will come out all high and squeaky."

"I have a friend who's a fantastic voice coach," Tj offered. "He's here tonight for the barbecue cook-off. I'd be happy to introduce you. Maybe he would be willing to listen to your song and give you some feedback."

"That would be great." Chloe smiled. "I have to check in with the group organizer, but I can meet you in half an hour."

"Perfect. I'll be up by the barbecue booths."

"Thank you so much." Chloe hugged Tj. "It was nice to meet you," she said to Jenna before trotting off.

"She seems nice," Jenna said.

"She is. She's a lot more serious than many of the girls. I hope she wins."

"If anyone can help her with her song, it's Kyle. The man is a miracle worker."

"Absolutely," Tj agreed. "I don't know what I would have done with my choir assignment if he hadn't offered to help out."

"So what's next on the agenda for the girls?" Jenna asked.

"There are evening gown and resort wear competitions this evening after the barbecue judging. This year each girl is judged in five outfits. Three are chosen by the Tropical Tan staff and the other two are chosen by the participants themselves."

"Wow, that's a lot of changing."

"Tell me about it. Each girl has someone assigned to help dress her so that everything moves along in an efficient manner. It's quite a production." Tj paused and looked around. "It looks like I've done what I can. Let's head over to the barbecue and root on the guys."

"Who do you think is going to win?" Jenna asked as they walked back across the resort.

"All the men who are entered have competed before and have made improvements to what seemed like perfectly fantastic recipes already. I think they should all win. I guess the judges will have to figure out some way to decide whose barbecue is actually the best."

"I think I'm going to have a bite of each one," Jenna decided. "Last year I filled up on Nolan's pork ribs because it was the first booth I visited. They were delicious, but I didn't have room to try anything else."

"Yeah, I've done that before too. I think I'm going to Jake's booth first. Hunter said Jake was pretty mad that he insisted on chicken over the usual ribs. I'm going to make a big fuss about how it's the best chicken I've ever tasted. I know Hunter is just trying to look out for his grandfather, but I feel bad for Jake. It must be hard to live with your doctor. Makes it almost impossible to cheat."

"I heard Jake was back in the hospital for a few days last month. How's he doing?"

"Okay, I guess," Tj said. "He had a second heart attack, but this one was mild. He's getting on in years and these things happen, but I know that, as his doctor and his grandson, Hunter wants to keep him healthy as long as he can."

"You know if you go over to his booth he's just going to try to convince you to marry Hunter while he's still alive to see it," Jenna warned her.

"I know. I wish it was that easy. There's nothing I'd like more than to make Jake happy. He's always been there for me. Almost like my own grandfather, although getting married to make him happy would be a bit extreme."

"Jake just wants you and Hunter to both be happy and settled. In his mind, the easiest way to accomplish that is to marry you to each other."

Tj laughed. "I know. Jake knows that things are a lot more complicated than he wants them to be. Personally, I think he just enjoys the banter. He calls me Hunter's girl and Hunter and I deny it. It's almost like some silly script we repeat over and over again."

"I bet that when he's gone, that silly script will be the thing you miss the most," Jenna speculated.

"You know," Tj felt her heart tighten at the thought of Jake not being there to tease her, "you could be right."

Echo decided to take a nap under the table Ben and Kyle had set up for distributing their ribs. Tj introduced Chloe to Kyle, who was more than happy to help her. Ben held down the fort while Chloe and Kyle wandered over to the bandstand where the competition would take place the following day to practice. Ben said he didn't need help, so Tj and Jenna wandered from booth to booth, speaking to each contestant and sneaking a taste of their entries. In the end, Doc and his melt-in-your-mouth brisket took the grand prize. All of the entries were delicious, and Tj was fuller than she could remember being in a long while by the time she invited everyone back to the house to talk about Roy's opinion on Tonya's death. Somehow, in light of the new evidence, it seemed like a good time to have a powwow to get everyone's input. Most of the people in town believed Tj was on a roll when it came to solving the unusual rash of murders in the area, but she knew that in every instance it had been a team effort.

"I can't believe you think we need dessert," Jenna commented as she helped Tj carry the three cheesecakes she'd snagged from the Grill on her way back to the house.

"Guys are guys. They always have room for dessert. I guess we should make some coffee."

"Is Jake coming over with Hunter? I doubt he's going to be allowed to eat cheesecake," Jenna pointed out.

"I had the chef make a special dessert for him. He'll love it, and there's nothing about it that Hunter could disapprove of. I guess we'll just plan to sit at the dining room table. If Hunter brings Jake and Doc brings Bookman, that will be six of us. I'm sure Kyle and Grandpa will come along, so let's figure on a total of eight. Let's set out eight cups and eight plates."

Tj hugged each man as he came through the door. She'd filled Doc and Hunter in on what was going on when she'd asked them to come over for dessert, so the conversation quickly moved on to the news Roy had shared with her concerning the autopsy report. The fact that Tonya had been found in the cove was now common knowledge, although the police were being selective in which details were made public.

"To be honest, I didn't look at the report all that closely," Hunter, who was sitting next to Tj, admitted. "I hadn't looked at it at all until Tj called me the other night. I skimmed down to the summary and left it at that. There didn't seem to be any question that the woman was murdered, and the blow to the head was evident to the naked eye. Not to take the easy way out, but reviewing autopsy reports isn't my job. I normally only look at them if asked to. Besides, it was the end of the day and I was tired."

"Why did Roy think the injury to the head might have been from a fall?" Bookman asked.

"One of the interns at the hospital saw the body and realized there might be another explanation than the one the coroner gave," Tj said. "She didn't have all the information and didn't want to make any enemies at the hospital by meddling in areas that weren't her concern, so she didn't want to bring it directly to the coroner's attention. She's a friend of Roy's and she knew he'd been at the scene, so she called him and asked some questions. Then Roy called the coroner, who insisted that his conclusion was accurate. When I spoke to Roy shortly after, he said he didn't want to get his friend the intern in trouble by admitting that she was the one who pointed him in that specific direction, so he asked me what I thought he should do. That's when I told him I'd ask you to take a look at the body." Tj looked directly at Doc.

"I think I know which intern you're referring to," Hunter added.

"She won't get in trouble, will she?" Tj asked.

"No. She's ambitious and hardworking and will make an excellent doctor. She's part of a tough rotation right now that puts her in the morgue two nights a week. Many interns wouldn't have bothered to read the report and look into things if something seemed odd. I admire her tenacity."

"Okay, so Doc will look at Tonya Overton tomorrow and we can figure things out from there," Tj said.

The room fell into silence for several minutes as the group wolfed down the dessert Jenna had served while they discussed the autopsy. Tj was glad she'd taken the extra effort with Jake's offering; he seemed touched by her thoughtfulness. Tj got up to refill coffee cups while Jenna cleared the dishes from the table. The rock and roll band had taken over and the warm sounds of familiar tunes in the background added a feeling of coziness to the evening. They were just finishing up when ex-deputy Nolan Rivers joined them.

"Would you like some dessert?" Tj asked Nolan.

"No. I just stopped by to fill you in on some interesting news regarding the dead woman." Nolan took a seat as the group waited for him to continue. "I probably shouldn't say anything, but it seems that the woman in the morgue isn't Tonya Overton."

"What?" Tj gasped. This whole thing was getting more and more bizarre. "If she's not Tonya Overton, who is she?"

"We have no idea."

Bookman's eyes lit up. If there was one thing the mystery writer loved, it was a good mystery. "What do you mean?"

Nolan hesitated. "If I tell you, it can't leave this room."

"Fine by me." Bookman sat on the edge of his chair. "What about everyone else?" He looked around the room, daring anyone to ruin his fun by suggesting that perhaps they shouldn't be having this conversation.

"We won't say anything," everyone agreed.

"After you asked Doc and Hunter to come by," Nolan looked at Tj, "I figured I still had enough pull down at the station to get some information, so I called the sheriff, who told me they had been looking for Tonya's next of kin since they found the body. Not only did they not find any family associated with the woman but, according to every record-keeping system they could think to check, the woman in the morgue doesn't exist."

"How can that be?" Jenna asked.

"There's a birth certificate, a social security card, and financial and employment history for Tonya Overton that goes back twenty-six years. But when they compared fingerprints and DNA to the body in the morgue, they don't match that of the real Tonya Overton."

"So the woman in the morgue stole Tonya Overton's identity?" Tj guessed.

"It appears so. The woman in the morgue began working for the Tropical Tan Corporation a year ago. The sheriff found an employment record stating that Tonya Overton worked for a travel agency two years ago. When the human resource director of the travel agency was shown our Tonya's photo, she said the woman in the photo and the woman who worked for them wasn't one and the same."

"So where is the real Tonya?" Jenna asked.

"Her location is unknown," Nolan stated. "The sheriff discovered that the Tonya Overton who worked for the travel agency moved out of her apartment within days of leaving her employment there. No one has seen or heard from her since. She was raised in foster care, has no family, and the few friends she had claim she simply dropped off the face of the earth."

"Was a missing persons report filed?" Jenna asked.

"No. The real Tonya quit her job, packed her stuff, and moved out of her apartment. She told friends that she needed to get away for a while but would keep in touch. She never did, but her friends assumed she'd simply moved on. According to what I could find out, she wasn't one to maintain close relationships."

"So if the woman in the morgue isn't Tonya Overton, who is she?" Jenna wondered.

"No one knows. Her fingerprints don't match any on file. The sheriff is still looking, but so far, no go."

"Maybe the new Tonya killed the real Tonya before assuming her identity, which is why the real Tonya never reappeared," Bookman suggested.

"Sounds like one of your thrillers. Dylan is going to be so mad that he's missing this interesting case," Tj said.

"Yeah, well, he might not be missing out for long. The sheriff told me that if they don't figure this out by the end of the weekend, he's going to revoke Dylan's leave. Roy and Tim are great, but they're homegrown deputies. They don't have Dylan's background or skill."

Having Dylan's leave revoked wouldn't go over well with his sister. She might even pack up her son and head home to Chicago before Dylan had the chance to talk her into staying. Tj didn't know if their relationship would ever evolve into anything more than a simple friendship, but she knew she'd like the opportunity to find out.

CHAPTER 14

Saturday, June 21

Saturday was the biggest day of the competition, with both the bathing suit and the talent contests. The girls were to walk the runway and pose for a photoshoot in four different bikinis. Two of the bathing suits had been selected by the company and the other two were the contestants' own choice. If history served, the suits chosen by the models tended to be little more than a few strings braided together. It was no wonder that the entire beach was crowded with spectators. Tj enjoyed the energy the bikini competition brought to the resort, but often, by the end of the day, this particular crowd tended toward rowdy displays of drunkenness.

"Someone is here to see you." Leiani walked into the Bar and Grill where Tj was helping Logan inventory the bar supplies in advance of the busy weekend with Annabeth trailing behind her.

"Good morning, Annabeth," Tj greeted the young girl. "Don't you look nice today?" Annabeth had combed her hair, washed her face, and dressed in clean but tattered shorts. Tj could see that she'd made an effort to look her best.

"I wanted to look nice in case you found Kiara."

"I'm sorry." Tj stood up. She'd been kneeling on the floor counting the bottles of rum in the locked cabinet behind the bar. "I haven't found her yet. Would you like something to eat?"

Annabeth looked toward the buffet breakfast that had been set out for the Tropical Tan staff and models. She seemed shy about answering, but Tj could tell she was hungry and very much wanted to accept the offer.

"Go ahead and help yourself. In fact, I'll join you. Logan can finish up here."

Tj and Annabeth each filled a plate and then went outside to eat in solitude. It was another sunny and warm day. Logan had built a fire in the pit on the deck, making it a toasty place from which to view the lake while dining. A lone coyote wandered down the beach, searching for remnants of food left behind by the previous day's crowd. A flock of geese took flight as the coyote neared, then landed again behind him as he continued on his way.

"You must have left early to be all the way out here by this time," Tj said as she spread boysenberry jam on a piece of toast.

"Papa didn't come home last night, so it was easy to sneak out," Annabeth answered with a mouth full of food.

"Does he do that often?" Tj asked. "Stay out all night?"

Annabeth shrugged. "Sometimes."

"It looks like you're enjoying those eggs." Tj chuckled as Annabeth shoveled the spinach scramble into her mouth.

"These are the best eggs I've ever tasted," Annabeth said. "Besides, Papa didn't leave any food in the house, and Nona wasn't home. I haven't had anything except some old crackers since I ate with you yesterday."

Tj frowned. "Does this happen often? Are you regularly left alone without food?"

"Papa usually keeps stuff around, but he's been gone more than usual lately. And I can usually go to Nona's, but she's been away as well. Can I have some more?"

"Absolutely. Get a new plate and help yourself."

Tj watched as Annabeth filled a second plate. It made her angry that a twelve-year-old girl would be left to fend for herself for such long periods of time.

As a schoolteacher, Tj had been forced to contact Child Protective Services a time or two, but more often than not, the child ended up worse off than before she'd called. Annabeth appeared to be a bright and independent girl who had figured out how to take care of herself, so for the time being, Tj decided to leave well enough alone.

"Whoever made these muffins is a genius," Annabeth stated when she returned to the table with a full plate, including several triple berry muffins, which were the chef's specialty. The muffins hadn't been on the menu the Tropical Tan staff had ordered, but Tj suspected they'd been added as a treat for the staff who stopped by to eat before beginning their shift.

"We have plenty because the models aren't apt to eat them," Tj responded. "How about I send some home with you?"

Annabeth smiled. "That would be awesome. Thanks."

"Did you manage to find out anything that might help us locate Kiara?" Tj asked.

Annabeth continued to shovel food into her mouth while Tj sipped her coffee. The poor thing must be starving.

"Not really," Annabeth answered. "Something is up, though. My dad is gone, Nona is gone, and Aaron is all secretive and quiet. I tried to ask him about Kiara, but he told me he had some stuff he needed to do and couldn't talk. He's usually nice about talking to me when I have questions and stuff. I'm pretty sure Kiara asked him to watch out for me before she left."

"So you think Kiara told Aaron that she planned to run away?" Tj was surprised by this bit of news.

"Yeah. Aaron and Kiara are friends. It was their dads' idea that they should get engaged, although I'm pretty sure Aaron would like to marry Kiara; he loves her, but he wants her to be happy. I'm pretty sure he figured that if he gave her space, she'd come back to him."

"But she didn't."

"Not so far. I'm not surprised, but I think Aaron is. Most girls in the settlement would be thrilled to get hitched to him. Can I have some more juice?"

"Sure. Do you have any idea where your dad and Nona might be?"

Annabeth sat back and looked at Tj. "My dad didn't say. He was gone when I got home yesterday, and I haven't seen him since. Nona left in the middle of the day. She said she needed to go into town for some supplies, but she hadn't come home by the time I left this morning. It's not odd for my dad to be gone for days at a time, but Nona usually comes home at night."

"Is there anyone else at the compound who might know where they've gone?" Tj asked.

Annabeth crossed her legs beneath her body and leaned back in the chair. She appeared to be considering the question. "My dad talks to Aaron and Aaron's dad sometimes, so I guess I can ask them if they know where he went. Nona doesn't talk to people much. At least not about where she goes when she leaves the settlement. She told me once that it's not anyone's business what she does with her time. Do you think I could stay here with you today?"

"Will you get into trouble?"

"I don't see how. Papa isn't around, and even if he comes back, he won't be looking for me. If I see Aaron or any of the other boys from the compound, I can duck out of sight. It sure would be fun to watch the models. Besides, maybe Kiara will come back today."

Tj hesitated. She didn't want Annabeth to get into trouble, but the poor girl could use a day of fun and relaxation. "Okay, you can stay for a while, but you have to promise me that you'll let me drive you home at the end of the day."

"I have my bike."

"We can put it in the back of my SUV."

Annabeth smiled. "Okay. What do we do first?"

"I need to call my dad and sisters to say hi and see how they're enjoying their vacation, but after that maybe we can go through some of my old stuff. I have a bunch of shorts and tops that I've been wanting to give away. Maybe you could help me out by taking some home with you."

"Really?" Annabeth's face lit up.

"It would be a huge help."

"Okay. Anything I can do. You've been so nice to me. Nicer than anyone other than Kiara. She brought me some clothes that a friend gave her a couple of years ago. I haven't had anything new since."

"A friend?" Tj asked. "Do you know the friend's name?"

Annabeth frowned. She bit her lip as she searched her memory. "Suzie," she finally said. "Her name was Suzie."

"Do you know her last name, or maybe where we can find this Suzie?"

"You think she knows where Kiara is?" Annabeth asked hopefully.

"It couldn't hurt to ask."

"One of the pairs of shorts had a name on the tag. I asked Kiara about it, and she said sometimes people put their name on the tag of their clothes when they go to camp. It would be fun to go to camp sometime. I don't know anyone who has actually gone, but one of the books Nona got for me was about a girl who went to camp, and it sounded fun to sleep in a cabin with other girls and tell stories by a fire."

"Did the tag have a last name?" Tj asked.

"Wallerman. Her name was Suzie Wallerman."

Luckily, not only did Tj happen to know Suzie Wallerman, but she knew where she lived. Tj left Annabeth in Amber's care with instructions to have her hair trimmed and nails groomed after she showered at the house and dressed in some of the clean clothes that Tj had managed to find in Annabeth's size.

Tj didn't think she'd be gone long, but she made certain Amber would not only keep an eye on the girl but make sure she got plenty to eat as well. Amber and Annabeth hit it off immediately. Amber said that Annabeth reminded her of the younger sister she'd left behind when she took the job at Maggie's Hideaway. However things worked out with Kiara, Tj suspected Annabeth had found a new friend in Amber for as long as both remained in the area.

Tj had looked up Suzie's number and called ahead. Suzie was twenty now. She'd graduated from Serenity High School a year ahead of Kiara would have if she'd attended. She was married now, with a four-month-old baby. Tj remembered that Suzie had dated the same boy all through high school. A lot of young marriages didn't work out in the long run, but Tj suspected Suzie's might. Both she and her husband, Kevin, seemed completely devoted to each other after getting off to a rocky start.

Tj stopped in at Grainger's General Store to buy a baby gift to bring when she called on the new mom. Grainger's was considered by most to be synonymous with the town of Serenity, a staple of the community for over fifty years. On any given summer day, the front deck was occupied by both visitors and locals, sitting at the tables provided for folks to gather around to enjoy a game of chess or checkers while sharing a pot of coffee and catching up on local news.

The store was laid out on two stories, the second being open in the center to the first. Wide stairs at each end of the building gave shoppers easy access to the clothing, camping supplies, and local souvenirs housed upstairs. Emma Grainger had added a new child and baby department the previous summer, so there was an entire corner on the second floor dedicated to everything for the twelve and under set.

Tj was trying to decide between an outfit and a stuffed animal when she noticed Hunter in the toy section, holding a stuffed dog as well as a stuffed lion.

"Picking out a new friend?" Tj teased.

"Actually, I'm trying to decide what to get for my cousin's new baby."

"I heard she had a little girl."

"Harmony," Hunter confirmed. "She really is the cutest thing. Lots of dark curls, blue eyes, and the sweetest smile."

"Sounds like someone might have a touch of baby fever," Tj observed.

"Me?" Hunter laughed. Tj loved the way his eyes crinkled in the corners when he smiled. "Hardly. I have to admit, though, the little vixen is only a month old and she's managed to pull a few of my heartstrings. I see babies in the hospital every day, but there's something about Harmony that makes me all gooey inside when I hold her."

"You do have baby fever," Tj accused. "If you were a woman, I'd say your biological clock was ticking loudly."

"So why are you here?" Hunter changed the subject. "A bit of baby fever yourself?"

"I'm looking for something for Suzie Wallerman's baby." Tj reached for a giant stuffed elephant that looked cuddly but wasn't.

"I wasn't aware you were friends with Suzie." Hunter replaced the lion, deciding on the dog instead.

"She was a student of mine the first year I taught at the high school. I've been meaning to get her something, but the main reason I'm going by today is because Annabeth mentioned Kiara and Suzie were friends."

"And you thought she might know where Kiara has run off to," Hunter concluded.

"At this point, I'm willing to pursue any lead that presents itself. I feel so bad for Annabeth. She's worried about her sister. The poor thing is only twelve, and it seems like she's basically raising herself. If I can find Kiara, maybe they can work out a way to be together."

"Do you think a big sister who just takes off is any better for Annabeth than what she already has?"

Tj paused. "Honestly, I don't know. I guess I just need to find Kiara and then figure out the rest. You know me; I like to nose my way into everyone else's problems."

Hunter laughed. "I promised my cousin I'd babysit Harmony this morning, but I'm free this afternoon. How about I come by the resort later and we put our heads together? A person doesn't simply disappear, and if what you say about Annabeth's relationship with her sister is true, she probably didn't just take off. There must be something we're missing."

"Thanks." Tj smiled. "I'd love to have your help. I think Kyle is coming by as well. Maybe between the three of us, we can put this mystery to bed."

Hunter looked disappointed that it wasn't going to be just the two of them, but after the dreams she'd been having since they'd spent time together on Wednesday night, she was happy to have a third person in the mix. The last thing she needed to add to her plate at the moment were messy emotions she had no idea how to deal with.

After agreeing on a time to meet up, Tj bought a gift and continued on to Suzie's.

"Coach Jensen." Suzie opened the door wide when Tj knocked. "Please come in."

"I brought a little something for Jason." Tj handed her the giant giraffe, which she realized might not have been the best choice for an infant. She'd thought about getting an outfit, but then she'd seen the giraffe and couldn't resist.

"That's so nice of you. Please have a seat." She motioned toward a sofa situated under a window in a clean apartment furnished with secondhand furniture. "The baby is sleeping right now, I'm afraid. I tried to keep him awake to meet you, but babies sleep when they get the urge, no matter how hard you try to distract them."

"I understand. I can always come back to meet him later. I apologize that I haven't been by before this."

"You've been busy with graduation and everything. You said you wanted to ask some questions about Kiara Boswell?" Suzie asked as she put the giraffe on the kitchen counter and sat down on a hardwood chair across from Tj.

"Yes. Kiara's sister, Annabeth, told me you know her. She's missing, so we're talking to anyone who might provide any information that will help us find her."

"We aren't really friends," Suzie informed her. "My

grandmother knows her grandmother. I was in the park one day and ran into my grammy. Nona was there with Kiara, and they introduced us. We talked while our grandmothers visited. I happened to mention that I had a bunch of clothes I wanted to get rid of, and Kiara was thrilled to take them off my hands. Nona followed us to my house and I gave her three or four bags of hand-me-downs. After that, I ran into Kiara in town a couple of times and we chatted for a minute, but that was the extent of our conversations. You said she's missing?"

"Yes. She got off the bus with the other models on Wednesday, but no one I've talked to has seen her since. When Annabeth told me that she received clothes from her sister's friend, I hoped you might know something that would lead to her whereabouts."

"I'm afraid I don't know anything. I haven't spoken to her in years. Have you tried talking to her grandmother? The two were really close."

"Yes, we've spoken to Nona. She didn't know where Kiara was either."

Suzie sat back in the chair, a look of concern on her face. "I hate to even consider the idea that something happened to Kiara, but she loved her sister. I can't imagine she'd be in the area and not check in with her."

"I'm afraid I've come to the same conclusion. If you think of anything, let me know."

"Have you spoken to Aaron? That's the name of the boy she was engaged to."

"I haven't seen Aaron around town, and it's pretty much impossible to get into the compound. Nona said she'd speak to him, but then she disappeared. Annabeth told me Aaron claims not to know where Kiara went after he left her on the beach."

"You know, you might talk to Travis Vidal. I know he's

friends with Aaron. It's a long shot, but I suppose a long shot is better than none at all."

"Do you have an address or phone number for him?"

"Yeah. Hang on, I'll get it." Suzie stood up just as the sound of a baby fussing in the background alerted them that Jason had awoken. "It sounds like Jason decided he'd like to meet you after all. Just give me a minute. I'll get the address and the baby."

Tj looked around the room while Suzie went to retrieve her crying infant. Tj wasn't sure she was quite ready for a baby, but she was open to the idea of one. Not that she had men lining up to take on the daddy role. Dylan had enough baggage to deal with that she doubted babies were anywhere on his radar.

And Hunter had denied having baby fever, but Tj had seen the look of longing in his eyes. There had been a time when she was certain she'd have Hunter's babies. She'd even picked out names: Hudson for a boy and Heather for a girl. She could remember scribbling the names in her diary when she was in high school. Then Hunter had ripped out her heart, and all of her thoughts of child rearing had been torn out with it.

"This is my big man." Suzie handed Tj the freshly diapered baby.

"He's adorable. He looks a lot like his daddy."

"Yeah, he's going to be a heart breaker," Suzie agreed.

"Is Kevin doing well as a daddy?"

"He really is. I was worried at first that my irresponsible husband would be a disaster as a father, but he's changed since the baby was born. He goes to work every day and comes home to Jason and me every night. At one point I thought I might have to raise my baby by myself, but now I believe we're going to make it."

"I'm so happy to hear that." Tj smiled.

After talking with Suzie, Tj promised to stay in touch and

then took her leave. She checked her messages when she returned to her car and found a voicemail from Dylan, asking her to call him. She hit redial and waited for him to answer. She'd found herself wishing she could ask his opinion about the mystery of the nameless girl in the morgue and was thrilled to have the opportunity to speak with him during his leave.

"Hey, Dylan. What's up?" Tj said when he answered.

"Justin saw a sign for the bikini contest when we were driving through town and wanted to attend today's festivities. I wanted to ask if it would be appropriate for children."

"I guess that depends. There are spectators of all ages, but many of the bikinis can be pretty small. I suppose it's a judgment call, although there are other things going on at the resort if you're uncomfortable with the way the women are dressed. And there are also events going on in town."

"I guess I'll talk to his mom about it. So how's the case coming along?"

Tj suspected that was his real reason for calling all along. "Not that I'm not happy to hear from you, but if you're curious about the case, why don't you just call Roy?"

"Because I'm on leave and he's in charge, and I don't want him to think I'm checking up on him."

"I have a feeling he might not mind a little checking up," Tj answered. "I know the guys didn't want to bother you while your sister was here, but things have gotten pretty complicated."

"Complicated how?" Dylan asked.

"For one thing, Tonya Overton isn't Tonya Overton."

"Come again?"

"The woman in the morgue has a driver's license and social security card that says she's Tonya Overton, but her fingerprints don't match those of the real Tonya Overton, who hasn't been seen or heard from for almost two years."

"So who's the woman in the morgue?" Dylan wondered.

"No one knows. Her prints aren't on file. Sheriff Boggs is looking into it."

Dylan sighed. "Maybe I should go in."

"Spend the day with your family," Tj advised. "The woman is dead; you can't help her. If they don't figure this out by next week, I think Boggs is planning to revoke your leave anyway."

"What about the missing model? Have you found her?"

"Not yet, but I'm working on it," Tj promised. "I have this gut feeling that all of this somehow fits together. I'm just not quite sure how yet."

"You know I think you should stay out of this and let Roy and the others do their job."

"I know."

"And you know I don't want you to get hurt."

"I do."

"But you're going to continue to nose around anyway."

"I am."

Dylan sighed. "That's what I figured. I hate that I can't be there to make sure you don't get yourself into trouble."

"Have I ever gotten myself into trouble?" Tj asked.

"Do you really want me to answer that question?"

"No, I guess not. I'm being careful."

"So what exactly do you know about this Tonya?"

Tj realized Dylan was frustrated by his inability to help out. Like her, he was the type who wanted to be in the thick of things.

"The woman in the morgue began working for the Tropical Tan Corporation a year ago. Boggs found an employment record stating that Tonya Overton worked for a travel agency two years ago, so whatever happened occurred in the year in between."

Tj filled Dylan in on everything she had learned, including

that the new Tonya appeared to have engaged in intimate relations with both Fenton and his son.

"Okay, so the real Tonya quits her job, packs up, and moves away, cutting off all ties with friends, and a different woman, claiming to be Tonya, uses her identity to get the job with Tropical Tan a year later," Dylan confirmed. "Once she begins working for the company, she has an affair with both the CEO and his son?"

"That's the way it looks. Bookman thinks the new Tonya killed the real Tonya before assuming her identity, which is why the real Tonya never reappeared."

"How did Bookman get involved in all of this?" Dylan asked.

"He attended our strategy meeting last night."

"You had a strategy meeting without me?"

Tj laughed. "Feeling left out?"

"Absolutely. If you come up with a name for the body in the morgue, call me. If I don't answer, leave a message and I'll get back to you. Things with Allie are sort of shaky as it is, so I'm trying not to mention murder investigations in her presence, though I'd like to stay involved. Have Roy run the prints of the body in the morgue through missing persons. If this woman has taken over Tonya Overton's identity, maybe someone is missing whoever it is she used to be. And make sure he checks into any Jane Does who might turn out to be the real Tonya. If Bookman is right and the woman in the morgue killed the real Tonya and took over her identity, then there should be a body somewhere. Oh, and check to see if the real Tonya ever reported any missing credit cards."

"Okay. I'll talk to Roy and keep you in the loop." Tj paused. "I miss you."

"Yeah." Dylan let out a long breath. "I miss you too."

CHAPTER 15

"So Travis didn't know anything?" Kyle asked later that afternoon. He'd come by to watch the talent portion of the competition.

"He said he hasn't talked to Aaron for over a week. He did tell me that Aaron cares for Kiara and would never do anything to hurt her. It sounds as if Aaron still hopes Kiara will follow through with the engagement, and Travis is certain that Aaron simply came to the resort to talk to her. He claims that Aaron isn't the sort to force her to do anything she doesn't want to do and believes he probably made his case and then left."

"Which leaves us back to square one," Kyle concluded.

"Pretty much, except Travis did think it was odd that Aaron hasn't been around," Tj said as she watched the models parade across the stage one by one as they were introduced. The crowd joined in by cheering for their favorite competitor, making it difficult to carry on a conversation. "They'd planned to attend the events at the resort together, but Aaron never showed. Like the rest of us, Travis can't just go to the settlement to check on things. Aaron always comes to him to make plans for future meetings. He wasn't overly worried, but he did say it wasn't like Aaron to simply flake on plans they'd made."

"Maybe Aaron is involved in Kiara's disappearance and is hiding out," Kyle said as the girls filed back off the stage in preparation for the individual demonstrations.

"Maybe. I sure do wish I could talk to him directly."

Tj watched as the first contestant filed onto the stage dressed in a leotard. The crowd quieted as she began a very complicated floor routine.

"And Nona never got back to you?" Kyle whispered. Luckily they were standing well behind the main body of the crowd so their conversation wouldn't be easily overheard.

"No, we haven't heard a word. When we talked to her, she said she'd talk to Aaron and let us know what he said, but she never contacted either Grandpa or me. According to Annabeth, Nona left Vengeance yesterday afternoon and as of this morning hadn't returned."

"Is Annabeth still here?"

"Yeah, she's hanging out with Amber. The pair are like two peas in a pod."

"Maybe you can ask Annabeth to talk to Aaron when she returns home. If he really is concerned for Kiara, he might let something slip."

The crowd cheered as the routine ended and contestant number one took a bow. The second contestant was the woman Tj knew as Jazzy. She was dressed in a tiny outfit that barely covered her critical parts. Her talent was listed as free dance but seemed more like something you'd see at a strip club. The men seemed to be loving it, as evidenced by the whistles and catcalls.

"I hate to even send her back until I know for certain that her dad or Nona are there," Tj said. She'd raised her voice slightly so she could be heard over the crowd. "She seems so self-sufficient, but she is only twelve. I'm concerned about her, especially because I can't just pop by and check on her whenever I want. Her dad left her alone overnight without any food in the house. What kind of a parent does that?"

"Get her a cell phone," Kyle said. "No one has to know she

has it, but if she has your number, she can call you anytime she needs to, and you can call and check on her."

"That's actually a good idea." Tj kissed Kyle on the cheek. "Thanks for the suggestion. I'll stop in town and get her one before I take her home. If she keeps it hidden and leaves the ringer on vibrate, no one will need to know she even has it."

"Oh good, here comes Chloe," Kyle announced. Chloe was dressed in a formal gown. She took a bow as the announcer explained that her talent would be to sing a ballad.

"Wow, she's good," Tj commented as Chloe began.

"She is," Kyle whispered. "When she first sang for me last night, she was so quiet that her voice didn't carry, but after we practiced I could see she had a lot of talent. If this bikini thing doesn't work out, I think she has what it takes to go pro."

"I know she really wants to go to college," Tj informed Kyle.

"Yeah, she mentioned that. She's a very mature and driven person. I'm sure she'll be successful at whatever she chooses to do. She reminds me a lot of Kendall."

"You still planning to help out with the choir next year?" Tj asked. Kyle should be the one acting as director, because he was musically inclined, while she decidedly wasn't.

"If you'll let me."

Tj laughed. "I'll more than let you. As far as I'm concerned, it's your baby. I'll help you where I can." Several of the teenage girls Tj had just waved to were whispering and glancing shyly at Kyle. If word got out that he was taking over show choir, she'd be willing to bet they'd get the bumper crop of new recruits needed since most of their strongest singers had graduated.

"I'm not a teacher," Kyle reminded her.

"You don't have to be. Show choir is designated as a club, so it isn't necessary to be certified to act as director. I'll run it past the administration, but I'm sure it will be fine."

"Deal." Kyle smiled. "Any word about the mystery of the body in the morgue?"

"Not really, other than that Doc looked at the body and agreed with the intern that Tonya, or whatever her name is, could very well have died as the result of a fall. If that's true, she may not have been murdered at all."

"So why would anyone tie her to an anchor and sink her?" Kyle asked. "If you're with someone and they fall and hit their head, why not call 911 to try and get help?"

"I don't have the answer to that question, I'm afraid. It seems like all we have are questions. And the longer this goes on, the more questions we have."

"Who is the woman in the morgue; how did she die; why did she assume someone else's identity?" Kyle counted off several of the questions they faced.

"That, and what happened to the original Tonya Overton and where is Kiara?"

"So what now?"

"I don't know. I guess my biggest concern is finding Kiara. I'm sure Roy is focusing on the woman in the morgue rather than Kiara, because a missing adult who might have left voluntarily isn't a huge priority."

"How is Roy doing with all of this?" Kyle asked.

"Honestly? I think he's in over his head."

"Yeah, I was afraid of that." Kyle sighed. "I understand why Dylan took leave at this particular time, but it would be nice to have him back on the job."

"I talked to him on the phone this morning," Tj said. "I think he's feeling pretty frustrated as well."

"And where has Sheriff Boggs been during all of this?"

Tj shrugged. "He's turned everything over to Roy, but he's also been putting up roadblocks to his investigation."

"How so?"

"By not letting him interview persons of interest. Boggs makes decisions based on the likelihood that a certain action will gain him attention and further his career. Indulgence is only on the other side of the lake, but if you want my opinion, as far as Boggs is concerned, we exist in a different world. A world he doesn't care about. He rarely makes the trip north unless something major is going on, which is fine if Dylan is around to oversee things. It's bad timing that his sister is here now."

"He's in a tough spot," Kyle admitted. "From everything I've heard, it seems important that this visit goes well."

"Wow, that's some costume." Tj directed Kyle's attention back to the competition. One of the women had opted to perform a ritual tribal dance and was outfitted in very little other than body paint.

"Yikes. Isn't this competition supposed to be family friendly?"

"You can't really see anything," Tj assured him.

"Maybe not, but it doesn't take a whole lot of imagination to fill in the blanks."

"I guess I see what you mean."

Tj was glad when the model was finished and the next one, another singer, took her place.

"What's on tap for the rest of the day?" Kyle asked.

"There's the main bikini competition this evening, as well as a good band I've been anxious to hear. Other than that, I figured I'd get Annabeth's cell phone and maybe nose around a bit. Hunter is going to come by later to help us come up with a strategy."

"Hunter has been around quite a bit lately."

"Yeah. We've been friends a long time, but we've become closer lately."

"I'm not sure you ever told me why you broke up in the first place."

Tj hesitated. Kyle had become one of her closest friends, but she hated to rehash painful memories. "Let's just say we were young, and Hunter's mother didn't approve of our relationship. Hunter is very much his own man now, but there was a time when he listened to his mother and tended to abide by her wishes. Who knows, maybe she wasn't wrong to be concerned that we'd become so serious at such a young age. I visited with one of my previous students today. She's only twenty now, but she's already married with a baby. It reminded me of Jenna, who married Dennis right out of high school. They're happy and have a wonderful family, but looking back, I'm not sure I was as ready for that back then as Jenna was."

"And now?" Kyle wondered.

"I wish I knew."

Kyle decided to hang out at the resort while Tj took Annabeth home. They planned to meet up with Hunter and Jenna to watch the swimsuit finals when she returned. As recently as two days ago, Tj hadn't cared who won, but now she was heavily favoring Chloe.

While the other girls were polite, they were also self-absorbed and dismissive. Chloe seemed to have a good heart and was the only one genuinely concerned about what had happened to Tonya and Kiara. And Chloe was humble. She didn't feel like the title was owed to her. She didn't even think she would win it. She was simply determined to do her best in the hope of getting the scholarship that she knew could change her life forever.

Annabeth seemed ready to leave when Tj suggested it, but

she hadn't said a word since they'd left the resort. Tj assumed Annabeth was tired after the long day, but she seemed contemplative as well.

"Anything on your mind?" Tj asked.

"Not really." Annabeth rolled down the window and stuck her head out like she'd seen Echo do. She seemed to enjoy the feel of the wind on her face. She closed her eyes and smiled as the wind whipped her hair. After a mile or so, she pulled her head in and leaned back into the seat.

"Is there anything you want to talk about?" Tj tried again.

"I was just thinking about stuff," Annabeth answered. "Do you think Kiara is dead?"

"No," Tj said with more certainty than she felt. "I don't know where she is or why we haven't found her, but I promise you that I'll keep looking until we do."

Annabeth looked out of the window. She appeared to be struggling with thoughts Tj could only imagine. It must have been hard to grow up in the environment she had. Tj's mother hadn't been in the picture, but she'd always had her father. She didn't know the entire story, but it didn't seem like Annabeth's father had much use for her at all.

"I think about her, you know," Annabeth said after a few minutes.

"Kiara?" Tj asked.

"My mom," Annabeth whispered. "I wonder where she went and whether she's happy and safe. Sometimes I imagine that she met a man and fell in love. I think about her coming back for me, bringing me to live with her new family. I think about a lot of things, but mostly I just wonder if she ever thinks of me."

"I'm sure she does. Just because she left doesn't mean she didn't love you."

"That's what Kiara says, but I wonder."

"Do you remember anything about your mother?" Tj asked.

"No. She left shortly after I was born. Nona told me she was young and scared and didn't know any better than to run away. Sometimes I wonder why she didn't take me with her. I wonder how my life would be if she had."

"Did Nona tell you anything at all about her?" Tj was curious about the circumstances that had resulted in Annabeth's birth and subsequent desertion by her mother. Maybe it was because she had been deserted by her own mother when she was three, which had left her with a deep-seated need to understand how such things could happen.

"I know her name was Katharine and she was very beautiful. She was raised in a very strict settlement from out of the area. Nona says that colony was even stricter than ours. When she was sixteen, she came to live with my father. Ten months later, I was born, and by the time I reached my first birthday she was gone."

"Do you know how your dad met your mom?" Tj wondered.

"I think theirs was an arranged union between their fathers. Things like that happen more often than you think."

Tj didn't think it happened all that often in this country, but she didn't say as much. Apparently, it was common among the group in which Annabeth had grown up.

"So Kiara would have been around six when your mom left. Did she remember her?" Tj turned off Main Street onto the highway heading north toward Vengeance.

"She told me she remembered small things about her. She remembered that she had a soft voice and a kind heart. She said she had long blond hair that hung past her waist and her smile made you feel welcome. Kiara told me that someday, when she got settled, she'd take me away from Vengeance. She told me she would help me look for my mom."

"I'm sure she will."

"Julie told me that your mother left you when you were young. That she married again and had two more daughters, and now they live with you."

"Julie is right. I was three when my mom left. Unlike you, who haven't seen your mom since you were a baby, I did see mine from time to time. But, like you, I wondered if she missed me and if she'd realize she'd made a mistake and come back for me one day."

"But she never did?"

"No, not really. Every now and then she'd visit, but once Ashley was born, she pretty much stopped doing that as well."

"Julie said your mom and her husband died. I guess your sisters must be orphans now."

"Actually, they're not." Tj wasn't sure why she was telling Annabeth all of this, except that she seemed vulnerable and it helped to share your feelings with someone who had been though a similar experience. "Ashley and Gracie were born to my mom and her second husband. They got divorced. My mom married for a third time, and that was the man who died in the accident."

"Their dad didn't want them?"

"He isn't in the picture," Tj explained. "He has some personal problems, so my mom left guardianship of the girls to me. I know he was notified when my mom died, but he's never contacted us."

Annabeth got a serious look on her face. "That's sad, but I guess it's good. I hope my daddy lets me go live with Kiara when we find her."

"Yeah," Tj sighed, "me too."

"This is it, up on the left. You can let me out here so no one sees you."

"Are you sure you want to go back? You can stay at the resort overnight if you want."

"No, I'll be okay. I want to see if Aaron is back. I want to ask him about Kiara. Besides, it sounds like Nona is back," Annabeth said as Tj pulled to the side of the dirt road leading to the village.

"How do you know?" Tj asked.

"Listen."

Tj did listen. There was a faint sound of chimes in the background. They seemed to be orchestrated into a regular pattern.

"The chimes are instruments Nona plays to calm her soul. If you hear chimes, you know she's at home."

"I'm glad she's back from wherever she was," Tj commented. "I feel better about leaving you with her around."

"I'm by myself all the time," Annabeth reminded her.

"I know. But now that I know you're here by yourself, I worry. Do you have the phone I gave you?"

Annabeth held it up.

"And you know how to use it?"

"If I need to talk to you, I just push the one. Your number has already been programmed in."

"That's right. And if you see that it's me calling, you press the green button like we practiced. If anyone else calls, just ignore it. I'm the only one who has your number right now. If you're in trouble and I don't answer, you can call 911. The person on the other end will help you. Do you remember how to call 911?"

"Of course, you dial 911."

"Yeah, I guess that was obvious. Sorry," Tj apologized. "I'm just feeling uncomfortable about leaving you."

Annabeth hugged Tj after she retrieved the girl's bike from

the back of the SUV and handed her the backpack she'd bought her to haul some of the clothes she'd given her to the settlement. "Don't worry. I'll be fine. I'm always fine," Annabeth assured her new friend.

Tj hugged the girl tightly. "If you can get away tomorrow, come by the resort. I should be there all day."

"I'll try."

CHAPTER 16

"I can't believe how many people came out for this," Kyle stated as hundreds of people crowded around the bandstand that had been set up on the beach.

"This is the final event," Tj explained as they walked past one of the four outdoor bars the resort had set up to handle the large crowd. "The girls have been trimmed from twenty-five—or twenty-four, given Kiara's absence—to ten. By the end of the night, they'll be down to five, who will be showcased tomorrow before the announcement is made. In the world of modeling, this is a big deal. Whoever wins this contest is going to get a lot of money and a jumpstart on their career."

"I'm glad Chloe made the final ten," Jenna commented as she nibbled on a steak kebab she'd purchased from one of the snack shacks set up on the grassy area behind the beach.

"I'm nervous for her," Tj added as the music began to play, indicating they were about to start. "To be honest, I didn't think she'd get this far. She's gorgeous and talented, but she's also sort of shy and a whole lot less flashy than the others. In my experience, flashy usually wins."

"What happened to the tall blonde with the surgically enhanced breasts?" Hunter shouted over the noise created as the crowd began to chant for the models to take the stage.

"That description applies to half of the women in the

contest," Tj pointed out. "Which surgically enhanced blonde were you referring to?"

"The one with the big hair and outrageous outfits," Hunter clarified.

"I assume you mean Jazzy. She didn't make the final cut, which is surprising considering she was last year's runner up and a heavy favorite," Tj said. "Although..."

"Although what?" Jenna asked.

Tj leaned in close and lowered her voice in spite of the noise around them. "It seems Jazzy and the CEO of the company's son have a thing going on. Or at least it seemed they did yesterday, when I happened to overhear a conversation they were having and observe a blatant walk of shame up to her room."

"You overheard a conversation they were having?" Hunter teased.

"Okay, I was spying. But I had good reason to. I thought either Fenton Ridley or his son, Porter, might have killed Tonya."

"Why is that?" Hunter asked as a teen with a corn dog almost ran smack dab into him as he darted in and out of the crowd.

"They both slept with her. Where have you been that you don't know that?"

"I've been here," Hunter pointed out. "I was here last night, and I don't recall you mentioning it."

"Oh. I guess it didn't come up."

"Do you still think one of the Ridley men is responsible?" Hunter asked.

"Honestly, no. With all the weirdness of this case, I think there's more going on than just love, lust, and revenge."

"You still haven't found out who the woman in the morgue is?" Jenna asked Hunter.

"Not as of a few hours ago," he confirmed. "Boggs did come in himself and take a look at the body, so I guess that's something. They're trying to match DNA, but nothing so far."

"Oh look, they're starting," Jenna interrupted.

"Ladies and gentlemen, meet your final ten for the Ms. Tropical Tan spokesmodel competition."

The crowd went wild as the ten finalists paraded onto the stage. The emcee introduced each one individually, providing her name and the town she represented.

Tj cheered as loudly as anyone when Chloe's name was announced. This evening was going to be the final bikini competition. Each model would walk the runway and then pose for a still shot in a variety of different swimsuits. Some had been chosen by the contestants, others by the company, but no two were the same.

"Chloe is the prettiest one," Kyle commented.

"Does someone have a little crush?" Tj teased.

"What? No. Chloe is much too young for me. I guess I'm rooting for her because she asked for my help with her singing. And," Kyle added, "she really is the prettiest one."

"Yeah, she is," Tj agreed.

Tj watched as each contestant was asked a question regarding the reason she wanted to be a Tropical Tan spokesmodel. It was a beautiful night, warm and calm, with a full moon glistening over the glassy lake. Bright lights had been strung through all the trees in the area, adding to the spotlights that illuminated the bandstand and the surrounding area.

Most of the models answered the question with totally bogus tales about bettering mankind and being a role model for today's youth. The well-rehearsed speeches were meant to sound authentic, but coupled with a teeny, tiny bikini, the answers seemed contrived at best.

Tj held her breath as Chloe was asked the standard question. She had on a dark green bikini that was well cut but modest and looked almost sophisticated compared to what some of the other girls were wearing. She had on high heels that looked impossible to walk in and a necklace with a solitary stone around her neck. While the majority of the girls had gone for flash, Chloe had chosen simple elegance.

"I want to be a doctor. In order to be a doctor, I need to go to a top-rated college. In order to pay for a top-rated college, I need the scholarship this contest provides. If chosen as this year's Ms. Tropical Tan, I'll work hard for the company during my reign and put the scholarship to good use."

Direct and to the point. Tj thought Chloe had given the only honest answer of the entire evening, but she doubted it would help her much with the judges, who were looking for tales of using suntan lotion to cure cancer or solve world hunger.

Once the question-and-answer period was over, a short break was called so the models could change.

"I could use a beer," Hunter announced. "Anyone else?"

"I'll go with you," Kyle offered.

"I'm good," Tj answered.

"Me too," Jenna added. After the guys walked off, she said, "I've been standing here appreciating this fantastic night and wondering what they would have done if it had rained."

"Panicked."

"That's it? You didn't have a plan B?"

"Actually, we didn't. I guess we would have tried to get as many people as we could fit into the community center. It wouldn't have been as awesome as standing out here under the stars, though."

"No, it wouldn't. Did Annabeth get home okay?"

"I dropped her off right before you got here. I hated to take her back, but I didn't want her to get into trouble if her dad realized she was gone."

"Was he there?"

"I'm not sure. Annabeth felt it was best that I leave off on the road, and she heard chimes and assured me that meant Nona was home. Still, I worry about her."

"It's such a shame she isn't able to go to school or have friends her own age. She's missing out on all the cool things that come with childhood."

"Yeah. I wish I could figure out a way to talk her dad into letting her go to school. Annabeth seems to think he won't even consider the idea. I've never spoken to the man, but based on what I've heard, I'm pretty sure she's right."

Tj waved to a group of her students who were attempting to make their way to the front of the crowd. They laughed and joked with one another as they shared the companionship of a night away from school, work, and other responsibilities. Tj wanted that for Annabeth. She wanted fun, friends, and normal.

"Isn't that Fenton Ridley arguing with Jazzy?" Jenna asked, interrupting Tj's thoughts.

Tj looked toward the tree line, where Fenton and Jazzy appeared to be in a heated conversation. Jazzy was wearing jeans and a halter top and looked quite a bit different than she had every other time Tj had seen her. Jazzy usually went for flare: big hair, lots of makeup, outrageous outfits. But tonight, without the trappings of her costumes, she seemed no different from the teens Tj worked with during the school year.

"That's him, but to be honest, I'm not sure I would have recognized her. She looks so different without the big hair and makeup."

"I only realized it was her because you can't help but notice her chest. Not a lot of women have that figure," Jenna said.

"I'm sure Jazzy isn't happy about not making the final ten."

"It looks like she's not the only one who's upset," Jenna said as Porter walked up, struck his dad in the face, and then walked away with Jazzy by his side.

"Yikes." Tj cringed. "Looks like Porter has a temper."

She thought about the comment Jazzy had made about Tonya making trouble for Porter by telling his father that he'd been sleeping with the models. Could Porter have killed Tonya to keep her quiet? Tj hadn't thought so before, but he obviously had a short fuse.

"I think I might call Roy and fill him in on the latest development," Tj informed Jenna.

"No need to; here he comes with Kyle and Hunter. He has his uniform on, and Tim is with him. I wonder if this is an official visit."

"I guess we're about to find out."

Tj watched as Roy changed direction and went over to speak to Fenton. Tj couldn't hear what was being said, but the conversation looked to be of a serious nature. After the men had finished their talking, Fenton signed something Roy handed him, and then Roy directed Tim to handcuff Porter, who was standing nearby with Jazzy.

Porter began yelling that his dad was setting him up as Tim cuffed him. He accused Fenton of covering his own butt as Roy joined Tim. After Porter was led away, Fenton returned to the bandstand and said something to the announcer, who instructed the band to start the music, announcing that the models would soon return to the stage.

"What the...?" Tj said. "Fenton had his son arrested for hitting him?"

"That just happened and Roy had to have already been here," Jenna pointed out. "It must be something else. Hunter and Kyle are on their way over. Maybe they know what's going on."

Tj watched the men approach.

"Quite the sideshow," Tj kidded. "What happened?"

"It seems Fenton called Roy a little while ago and told him he had reason to believe his son had killed Tonya Overton. He didn't want to come in for an interview since he needed to be here for the bikini contest, but he provided some information over the phone and then signed an affidavit stating that Porter and Tonya were having an affair and he suspected his son of getting mad and killing her when she broke things off."

"Wow. I honestly have to say I didn't see that coming," Tj commented. "I mean, I guess the thought had entered my mind when I realized Porter had a grudge against Tonya, but somehow the whole thing seems too easy."

"Why easy?" Jenna asked.

"I don't know. Maybe convenient is a better word. Did Fenton say what proof he had?"

"Roy didn't tell us," Hunter answered. "I imagine they'll get this all sorted out once the competition is over."

"Does this whole thing seem sort of cold to you?" Tj asked.

"Cold how?" Kyle wondered.

"Fenton calls Roy and reports that his son murdered a woman he professed to be friends with right up until her death. He wants his son arrested but can't be bothered to go down to the station to make a formal complaint. I get that this contest is important, but there are plenty of Tropical Tan people on-site to make sure the pageant goes off without a hitch. Fenton didn't even seem upset. He just signed the paper, watched Roy lead his son away, and went back to work."

"Yeah, I guess when you put it like that, it does seem sort of cold," Kyle agreed.

"Roy's original intel was that it was Fenton who had an affair with Tonya. What if Fenton is setting Porter up to take the fall for something he did?"

"I doubt any father would do such a thing," Jenna said.

"Fenton left Porter's mother when he was two. He didn't see him again until Porter turned eighteen and sought him out. He doesn't have a great track record as a father. I overheard the other day that Tonya had gotten Porter into hot water with his dad. What if Tonya went to Fenton and threatened to go public with the information that his son was sleeping with half the contestants? He kills Tonya and then frames his son."

"I don't know, Tj," Hunter responded. "Seems sort of farfetched."

CHAPTER 17

Sunday, June 22

"Annabeth?" Tj squinted to look at the bedside clock in the dark room. Normally she turned off her cell phone at night, but she'd had a missed call from Annabeth earlier in the evening and hadn't been able to get hold of her when she'd called her back. She'd never even known of the girl's existence a week ago, but now she worried about her as if she were one of her own. Tj wasn't sure what she was going to do about the fact that Annabeth seemed to be left to her own devices far too often for a girl of her age, but she'd made a personal commitment to help her in any way she could.

"I'm sorry to call so late," Annabeth whispered.

Tj sat up in bed. The moon shining over the lake was almost full, giving off a decent amount of light, so she didn't have to turn on the table lamp. The clock on her nightstand informed her that it was a quarter past one in the morning. Cuervo yawned, stretched his long limbs, and then circled the area until he found a location to his liking before curling up at the foot of her bed and going back to sleep. Echo had yet to be disturbed by the late-night call and was snoring soundly next to the bed.

"That's okay." Tj pulled the sheet over her shoulders as a breeze from the lake blew in through an open window. "I saw that you called earlier. I guess I didn't hear the phone with the band and all. I called back, but you didn't answer."

"I had to turn the phone off for a while so Papa wouldn't hear me talking. He came home right after you dropped me off. He noticed my haircut and new clothes and was mad that I'd left the settlement, so he locked me in my room. I tried to get out, but the door is locked and he blocked the window from the outside."

"He locked you in your room?" Tj was appalled. What if there was a fire?

"It's not so bad. He was drunk, and I'm sure as soon as he sobers up he'll let me out. Besides, I'd actually prefer to stay in my room, out of his way. The thing is, Aaron came over earlier and I heard them talking." Annabeth was whispering, so Tj had to concentrate to make out her words. "He was really mad."

"Aaron?" Tj clarified.

"Yeah. He was arguing with my dad. I think they forgot that I could hear them through the door. Aaron might not have even known I was in the house. Anyway, Aaron shouted that they couldn't keep her in there forever. I knew they were talking about Kiara. Aaron wanted my dad to let her go, but my dad refused. He told Aaron that it was a father's responsibility to do what was right for his child."

"Including kidnapping?" Tj had a hard time wrapping her head around the whole idea. Kiara was eighteen and, by law, free to do as she chose, whether her dad agreed with her choices or not.

"Papa doesn't see it that way. He says Kiara doesn't know what's good for her. He told Aaron that once they broke her, she'd go along with the plan and everyone would be happy."

"Broke her? Do you think they're hurting her?"

"I don't know. I don't think she's in physical danger. I'm pretty sure if she was, Aaron would break her out whether it made my dad mad or not. I'm guessing they're just keeping her locked up until she cooperates. At least that's how it sounded, although I can't be sure."

Tj tried to collect her thoughts. If Kiara was in trouble, she needed to do something to help her. Problem was, she had no idea what that something should be.

"What did Aaron say after your dad mentioned the need to break her?" Tj asked.

"I could tell he was uncomfortable about them keeping Kiara locked up, but I also think he's scared of Papa. Aaron is a big man who is young and strong, but he's a gentle person. He tends to go along with the older members of the community."

"How old is Aaron?" Tj asked. She couldn't remember if anyone had actually mentioned it.

"I'm not sure, but I think he's a little older than Kiara. Maybe two or three years."

"Okay, go on. What did Aaron say after your dad told him he wasn't willing to let Kiara go yet?"

"Aaron agreed to give it a few more days. I could tell he was reluctant, but Papa is a leader in the settlement and most of the younger guys don't like to cross him. Papa is known for his temper."

"Is that it?" Tj slipped out of bed and began pulling clothes out of the closet. She wasn't sure what she was going to do, but she couldn't just go back to sleep with both Kiara and Annabeth locked away by a madman.

"Aaron left after that, and I think Papa might have drunk the rest of his whiskey and passed out. Either that or he left again. I can't see into the other room, but it's real quiet."

"How can I help?" Tj asked. "Is there a way I can sneak into Vengeance and help you get out? Maybe I can unblock the window from the outside." Tj hated to think of the poor girl locked in her room with no means of escape.

"I'm okay, but I'm worried about Kiara. My dad can be mean when he's been drinking, and I could tell that his argument with Aaron got him all worked up. Before it got quiet there was a lot of pacing and cussing. I've been trying to figure out where he might have taken her, and I think I might know. I realize it's a lot to ask, but I was hoping you'd take a drive out and look."

"Absolutely. Just tell me where to go," Tj agreed.

"There's a cellar about a quarter of a mile behind the main compound. It's almost completely underground except for a very small window that sticks up about a foot above the surface of the ground. There are a lot of shrubs growing around it, so it's hard to see unless you know it's there. The door is at the end of a narrow path that's dug into the earth so that the entrance is actually below the ground. The room is probably locked, but I figure if you can look in the window and see Kiara, then maybe you can get help to get her out."

"Is the cellar being used for some purpose?" Tj wondered if others from the settlement might know of Kiara's presence if that was where they'd stashed her.

"No," Annabeth said. "It was built a long time ago by some guy who thought we were going to get bombed and wanted a place to take his family. They used to store supplies down there, but it's been completely abandoned since I can remember. I used to play there as a child."

It was incredibly sad that Annabeth no longer thought of herself as a child.

"I think most people have forgotten it even exists,"

Annabeth continued. "I know Papa remembers it, though, 'cause he caught me playing there a few years ago. He told me it was dangerous and made me promise to stay away, but I couldn't help myself and went back whenever I could."

Tj tried to picture where the cellar might be located. "Is it directly behind the compound?"

"It's sort of northwest. It'll be hard to find, but I think it's going to be easier to rescue Kiara when it's dark. Come morning, someone from the settlement is sure to see you."

"Okay. Tell me what to do and I'll do it."

Tj drove slowly through town. It was the middle of the night and there wasn't a single car on the road. The moon helped illuminate the landscape, which was going to come in handy once she reached the dirt road Annabeth had instructed her to turn onto. The emptiness of Serenity made her feel like she was the last survivor in one of those disaster movies in which only the buildings survive. The street was totally quiet and dark except for the security lights that shone from several of the storefronts.

As she turned off Main Street onto the highway leading north, she wished she'd been able to bring Echo, but Annabeth had warned her that she'd need to climb a fence in order to reach her destination. She'd have preferred to have him along for protection, but had decided to leave him safely at home where he wouldn't get hurt.

She hadn't wanted to worry her grandfather and figured she'd be home long before he woke up, so she'd sneaked out of the house as quietly as she could. She realized after she was already on the road that she should have left a note in case he got up in the middle of the night and noticed she wasn't there.

With the crowning of Ms. Tropical Tan that afternoon, there was a good likelihood he'd be up earlier than usual.

The narrow two-lane highway leading north out of the basin was deserted, as the town had been. Tj kept her eyes focused on the landmarks she passed as she neared the turnoff to the compound. Annabeth had instructed her to look for a poorly maintained dirt road about a hundred yards before the settlement. She was to turn off her headlights so as not to draw attention to herself and then drive slowly until she came to a chain-link fence. Annabeth had suggested she park in the trees so her vehicle wouldn't be seen and then continue on foot.

Tj slowed as she hunted for the turnoff. If she'd been traveling any faster, she would have missed it completely. The dirt road Annabeth had referred to was really two wheel tracks overgrown with weeds. Tj turned off her headlights and inched along the trail as Annabeth had instructed. Although it was late, Annabeth had warned her that if anyone from Vengeance saw headlights, they'd almost definitely come looking for the source.

Rubbing her eyes in an effort to focus, Tj found herself wishing she'd had an earlier night. The truth of the matter was that she'd only been sleeping for about an hour when Annabeth had called, and she was beyond tired. She thought of turning on the radio for company but realized that the sound might carry, alerting anyone who might be watching that she'd wandered onto private property. The signs she passed warned that unauthorized visitors would be shot on sight. Tj hoped that was a scare tactic and not a reality, even though she planned to be long gone before anyone noticed her.

Deciding to think about something other than a shotgun pointed at her face, she tried to re-create the evening she'd had in her mind. She'd had a wonderful time with Hunter, Kyle, and Jenna. After the bikini contest, they'd drunk wine and eaten festival food as Tj, Jenna, and Hunter spent hours next to the fire pit on the deck of the Grill, telling Kyle tales from their childhood. It had been fun to take a walk along memory lane. The two had been such an important part of her life for so long that at times, Tj realized, she tended to take them for granted.

Kyle fit in so perfectly with the group that Tj often forgot he was relatively new to town and didn't know the history behind many of the stories they shared. After tonight, Tj grinned, there were very few secrets left untold. Tj couldn't remember the last time she'd laughed so hard or had such a good time. She and Hunter had gone through rough times, but over the course of the evening, she'd had a chance to remember the good times as well.

The SUV hit a bump, causing Tj to refocus on the road. At the pace she needed to travel to keep the vehicle centered on the narrow road, she figured she could make better time walking. She found a good place to stash the SUV and took off down the dark trail on foot. It was a warm evening as mountain nights went, but still the air was nippy, and she wished she'd thought to wear a heavier sweatshirt. As she ambled down the rutted trail, an owl hooted in the distance. The sound of a lone owl had always seemed a lonely call to Tj. She listened as other nocturnal predators scurried in the dense foliage on either side of the trail. There was a slight breeze, causing the branches of the densely populated trees to creak and groan and giving the late-night adventure a spooky feeling that would be perfect if it were Halloween.

Before long, she came to the fence Annabeth had warned her about. It was tall, at least twelve feet. She didn't think she'd have a problem scaling it, but if she did manage to rescue Kiara and she was injured or in some way incapacitated, she had no idea how she'd get them both over the fence on the return trip.

Deciding she'd cross that bridge if and when she got to it, she began her climb up and over the top. Luckily, she'd worn long pants, long sleeves, and sturdy shoes. She wished she'd thought to bring gloves when she saw the barbed wire wrapped around the top. By the time she made it to the other side, her hands were bleeding, but she carried on according to the directions she'd received.

Tj almost jumped out of her skin when a pack of coyotes crossed her trail and began to yip and holler as they noticed her. She searched for a large stick she could use to fend them off if need be. There were a lot of coyotes in the area and most wouldn't attack an adult, but a whole pack on a dark night with a single human interrupting their nightly forage for food provided an uncertain situation at best. Tj stood still as the animals paused to watch her. There were six in all, most likely a family that hunted together. Their bright eyes looked eerie in the darkness, but the likelihood of them attacking if Tj didn't pose a threat was slim. She held her breath as they circled her, yipping and hollering all the while. She was small by human standards but still large enough to pose more of a problem to coyotes looking for a meal than would be worth the effort to attack...she hoped.

After several minutes, the animals regrouped and continued on their way. Tj located a large stick in case they returned and then continued on hers. Annabeth had said that she should be able to make out the edges of the cellar once she'd been walking for ten or fifteen minutes. She hadn't thought to actually time herself, but she figured that if she deleted the time she'd waited for the nocturnal prowlers, she must be nearing the bottom edge of the time range. Annabeth had mentioned that there would be a large tree with multiple trunks that wound their way around each other, as if they were embracing. Once she saw the tree, she was to continue another hundred yards to the left. And when she'd traveled the length of a football field, give or take, she would see a grove of aspens with thick underbrush. She was to continue on a narrow footpath that wound along the perimeter of the grove until she came to an area where large boulders blocked her passage. If she looked to her right, she should be able to see the top of the structure. It was dark brown and, as such, well camouflaged, but Annabeth had assured her that if she looked closely, she'd see the small windows that provided daylight to the underground room.

Tj walked carefully along the path strewn with debris. She noticed that there were several sets of footprints that looked like they'd been left recently. Definitely, she decided, since the last rain. The underbrush was dense, making it hard to make out a specific area where the cellar might be located. She recited Annabeth's instructions in her mind and then paused to scan the area. A twig snapped in the distance, causing Tj to hold her breath as she listened. It was probably just a forest animal out for a stroll, but the eerie setting of her late-night mission made her heart race with each and every noise.

She'd pretty much decided to check out a particular clump of shrubs when she heard something behind her. She turned to look, but before she could focus her eyes, everything went black.

CHAPTER 18

The first thing Tj realized as she struggled toward consciousness was that her whole body hurt. Her head throbbed worse than it ever had before, including the morning after her twenty-first birthday, when she'd gotten drunker than she'd ever been before or ever would be again. She felt as if one or more of the ribs on her right side might be broken, and she was certain that the numbness in her legs was the result of some horrible injury. She was lying on something hard and cold. So very, very cold. She struggled to open her eyes, but her eyelids felt heavy. She was trying to move one leg to see if she could when she heard a voice.

"Are you awake?"

The voice seemed to be coming from far away. Beyond the fog that prevented her from continuing into the realm of consciousness. The harder she tried to move toward the sound of the voice, the heavier her legs felt. Tj had had dreams like this; dreams in which she knew she had to escape, but her legs wouldn't cooperate. She knew she had to be dreaming, but this time it felt different. This time it felt real.

"Please don't die." The voice beckoned her from beyond the fog. "I know it's hard, but you need to wake up."

The voice sounded desperate. Tj tried to identify it, but the pounding in her head drowned out everything else. She knew the easiest choice was to give in to the darkness. In the darkness, there was no pain. In the darkness, she'd find peace.

"I'm so scared. Please wake up," the distant voice pleaded.

Tj made a decision and headed toward the voice. Each step caused her head to vibrate with a pounding that wouldn't stop. Her legs felt like lead, but still she struggled forward. When it seemed she could go no farther, she stepped into the light at the end of the trail.

"Thank God you're alive."

Tj slowly opened her eyes. Kiara sat next to her, sobbing, as she wiped her hair from her face. Tj struggled to focus in the dimly lit room. Her head hurt so badly that she had to use every ounce of willpower she possessed not to slip back into the fog.

"Where are we?" she asked.

"An old bomb shelter."

Of course, the shelter. Everything was beginning to come back to her now. She'd come into the woods to look for the cellar. Someone must have followed her. Tj tried to sit up, but the pain in her head was too intense. She closed her eyes and laid back down on the hard surface beneath her. "How long have I been here?"

"Several hours, I think. Maybe more. I don't have a way to tell time, so it's hard to know."

"Annabeth?" Tj asked.

"I don't know. They only brought you. They didn't say anything about Annabeth."

Tj opened her eyes. She tried again to sit up. It hurt a little less this time. "Who brought me? You said they brought me. Who is they?"

"Papa and Mr. Ward."

"Aaron's dad?"

"Yes."

Tj sat up and leaned against the wall behind her. She touched her forehead and felt her hair matted with a wet substance, most likely blood. The room she and Kiara were trapped in was made up of a cement floor and walls. There was a small window at the very top of the room to let in just enough light to make out the shapes of objects. There was a cot with a heavy blanket and a bucket, which Tj guessed served as the latrine. There was little else except the stairs that led upward to a doorway.

"It's locked," Kiara told her.

"And the window?"

"Bars on the outside. We can't get out. Believe me, I've tried."

"You've been here since Wednesday?"

Kiara nodded.

"Have you been given food and water?"

"They come by twice a day with food and water."

Tj closed her eyes and considered the situation. If whoever had hit her in the head meant to kill her, she'd be dead. There was no reason to bring her here only to finish the job later. The room they were trapped in was cold and dismal, but if they'd intended to kill Kiara, they would have already done so. The fact that they were feeding her showed that they intended to keep her alive.

"How did you find me?" Kiara asked. "I saw you walking toward me and then I saw Papa and Mr. Ward."

"Annabeth called me."

"She called you?"

"I gave her a cell phone so she could get hold of me when she needed me. She told me she heard Aaron and your dad arguing. Aaron insisted that they couldn't keep you locked up forever. He wanted to let you go, but your dad refused. Annabeth remembered playing near this place, so she called and asked me to come out and look through the window. I was supposed to rescue you, but I guess that didn't turn out all that well."

Kiara gently brushed Tj's hair from her face. "Annabeth shouldn't have gotten you involved. She should have known something like this would happen."

Tj winced as she shifted her position. Her head felt like it had been split in two. "She's scared for you. She came to the resort to see you, and when she couldn't find you, she panicked. We've been looking for you ever since."

"You're from the resort?"

"Yes. My name is Tj."

Kiara leaned against the wall and began to cry. "I can't believe how messed up everything has gotten. I'm so sorry you've been hurt. This whole mess is my fault."

"Perhaps you should tell me what you know," Tj prompted.

"It's kind of a long story."

Tj looked around the room. There was absolutely nothing to do and no way out. "It appears my day has been freed up. How about we get up off this cold floor and sit on the cot," Tj said.

Kiara helped her stand. Tj felt like she might faint or vomit, or both, when she first tried to get up, but somehow she made it to the cot. Kiara insisted she lie down. After covering her with the blanket, Kiara sat on the cot at her feet with her back against the wall.

"It seems you already know quite a bit," Kiara began.

"I know that your name is Kiara Boswell. You grew up in Vengeance and became involved in an arranged engagement to Aaron Ward. I know you ran away about a year ago and in that time somehow managed to become involved in the Ms. Tropical

Tan competition. I know Aaron met you at the bus and you left with him. No one has seen you since. Beyond that, I don't know a whole lot. Why don't you fill in some of the blanks?" Tj grimaced as her head began to pound even worse than it had before.

"I don't know where to start."

"How about the beginning?" Tj suggested.

"My mother died giving birth to me," Kiara began.

Tj didn't mean that far back, but she figured it couldn't hurt to keep Kiara talking. If nothing else, her story would provide a distraction to the pain her entire body was feeling. She hoped the pain she felt was due to bruising and not a more serious injury. In addition to the throbbing in her head, her leg was bleeding, and she was fairly sure that several of her ribs were bruised.

"There are those in the village I grew up in who believed that her death was my fault," Kiara began. "Like I was some kind of demon who killed my own mother when I came into the world. My father didn't want anything to do with me, so he gave me to Nona, which I might add, was the luckiest thing that ever happened to me. Nona is different from the others. She chooses to stay in the village for reasons of her own, but she's not of the village, if you know what I mean."

Tj believed she did.

"Nona taught me how to read and introduced me to a world beyond the walls of Vengeance. For as long as I can remember, all I've ever wanted to do was leave. With Nona as my unofficial guardian, I believed that was possible."

"And then your dad decided you should move back in with him." Tj decided it was time to bring the story around to the present.

"Exactly. Worse than that, he arranged for me to be

married to his friend's son. I like Aaron; I really do. He's sweet and gentle and seems to genuinely care about me. But I don't want to be married to him or anyone else."

"So you ran away."

"Yes, I ran away. It was hard. Really hard. I didn't have any ID. I was born at home, so I never had a birth certificate. I never went to school or visited a doctor or got a driver's license. The only job I could get was at a dive diner in Los Angeles, where the owner was willing to pay me under the table and didn't seem to care whether I had a social security number or paid taxes." Kiara stopped to catch her breath.

"Go on," Tj encouraged.

"About five months ago, a woman came into the diner. I knew right away it was Annabeth's mother, Katharine. She had dark hair, while Katharine was blond, and was going by the name Tonya, but when she smiled, I knew it was her."

Oh God. The dead woman was Annabeth's mother. Poor Annabeth. She'd never known her mother, so one might assume that the news of her death would be anticlimactic, but Tj knew that just because your mom leaves you behind, it doesn't mean you stop missing her.

"We got to talking, and Katharine told me how desperately she wanted to rescue Annabeth from our father," Kiara continued, oblivious to Tj's distress. "She had been living on the street in Miami and didn't have any money or transportation to make the trip west, so she came up with a plan. Katharine heard about the bikini contest several months before we met. She knew that the finals were to be held in Serenity, so she'd used her friend's ID to get a job with the Tropical Tan Corporation. She was in Los Angeles for a seminar when we ran into each other."

"The real Tonya Overton was Katharine's friend?" Tj

realized that she'd become distracted by thoughts of Annabeth's grief and needed to catch up.

"Yes. They met when they both lived on the street. Katharine faced the same obstacles I had when she left Vengeance. She effectively had no past. It's very difficult to get a job and a place to live with no form of identification."

"There are people who make fake IDs," Tj pointed out.

"Sure, for a lot of money. Katharine didn't have any. She told me that when she left Vengeance, she intended to come back for Annabeth, but the years slipped away. When I recognized her, she began to cry. She didn't even realize that Annabeth was almost a teenager. It's easy to lose track of time when you're living on the street."

"So back to the real Tonya Overton..." Tj persuaded.

"Tonya was a drug addict," Kiara continued. "She'd had a good job until she got into heroin and ended up a total mess. I guess she quit her job and took off when things got too intense, and at some point, she ended up in the same homeless shelter as Katharine. They became friends. Tonya got sick and knew she was going to die. In the end, she told Katharine to use her ID to get a job so she could go find her little girl."

"And the real Tonya's family?" Tj asked.

"She grew up in foster care and didn't have anyone."

"And after you met Katharine...?"

"She said she could get me an audition for the bikini contest. We figured if we both went to Serenity we could work together to liberate Annabeth from the village. Besides, if I won the contest, I'd have money for us all to start over. Katharine said she could arrange it so that I made it to the final twenty-five. I'd have to place in the top five on my own, but Katharine was certain that goal was within my reach. She helped me with my hair and makeup, and somehow she scraped together enough money for me to get the headshots I needed. I didn't have a car or money for a cab so I walked everywhere I went. I was in pretty good shape, but I needed a tan, so Katharine found a tanning salon that was willing to sponsor me."

"So you made it to the top twenty-five and came to Maggie's Hideaway," Tj urged. "I assume something went wrong."

"Katharine had to attend some sort of meeting at the Tropical Tan headquarters in Miami," she explained. "She was supposed to meet us at the bus and make the trip to Maggie's Hideaway with us, but she never showed. When I got off the bus and saw Aaron waiting for me, I panicked. He said there'd been a change of plans, but that he'd take me to Katharine. I was surprised Katharine let him in on our plan, but I figured she had her reasons so I went with him."

"And then?"

"After we got down to the beach, I began to get suspicious. Something seemed off. If Katharine couldn't come to the resort for some reason, why not meet me on the beach? Why the cove? I wanted to go back to the resort, but Aaron assured me that meeting Katharine in the cove was the only way to ensure Annabeth's safety. So I followed him."

Kiara stopped and took a breath. She appeared to be gathering her strength to continue. Tj realized that whatever happened to Tonya happened in the next moments of the story. Tj hated to make Kiara relive those horrible memories, but sometimes talking about what had happened was the only way to exorcise the memories that haunted you.

"When we got to the cove, Katharine was there to meet me, as promised, but my dad and Mr. Ward were there too, waiting on a boat." Kiara began to sob. "She said she was sorry. She said they'd threatened to hurt Annabeth if she didn't cooperate. She was crying, and I knew that she felt trapped by the situation. My dad demanded that I get into the boat, but I refused. He jumped onto the beach and grabbed my arm. I tried to get away, but he picked me up and hauled me onto the deck."

Kiara put her head down.

"You can stop if you want," Tj offered.

"No, it's okay." Kiara took a deep breath. "Katharine climbed aboard and demanded to be taken to Annabeth. She was upset and kept saying that she'd done her part and wanted her child. My dad just laughed and said she'd never see her daughter again. He shoved her off the boat and she hit her head on a rock. I screamed, but there was no one to hear me. Aaron tried to save her, but she was already dead. My dad, calm as could be, tied her to the anchor, took her out to deeper water, and let her sink to the bottom. Then he brought me here, and I've been here ever since."

So Fenton had lied about his son's part in Tonya's death, Tj realized, just not for the reason she'd suspected. If neither Fenton nor Porter had killed Tonya, what possible reason could Fenton have had for turning Porter in to the sheriff? Fenton had told Roy he had proof of his son's guilt, which was impossible if Porter was innocent. Tj suspected there was a lot more to that story than any of them realized.

"Do you know why they're keeping you here?" Tj asked.

"They want me to have a child. Aaron's child. Some Gypsy fortune-teller told my father that we would have an offspring with great power. Children are a commodity to people like my father. A grandson who's believed to possess some great supernatural abilities would bring him a certain level of prestige. They're planning to keep me here until I come to my senses and have the child they feel I am destined to bear."

"If Aaron loves you, why doesn't he help you escape?" Tj wondered. She yawned and snuggled closer to Kiara.

"Aaron is sweet but simple. I doubt he has what it takes to defy his father. And, like our fathers, he believes we're destined to have a child who will do great things."

"Hmm."

"Are you going to sleep?" Kiara demanded.

"Just resting my eyes," Tj said.

"You can't go to sleep. You probably have a concussion. You need to stay awake until we figure out how to get out of here."

Tj sat up and looked around the room. "Annabeth has a phone. I'm sure she'll call 911 when I don't get in contact with her."

"I hope so."

"So you want to be a doctor?" Tj knew it was best to keep talking.

"It's the only thing I've ever wanted, other than to live my own life and help Annabeth do so as well. I know it'll be tough. I have absolutely zero formal education. I know that I can take an equivalency test, and I'm fairly certain I can pass it, but I still have to convince a decent college to take a chance and let me in. And even if I get in, there's no guarantee I'll be able to pay my tuition. Winning the bikini contest was always a long shot, but now...Besides, I won't leave Annabeth again," Kiara stated definitively. "I never should have in the first place. I thought I'd be back for her within a matter of weeks. Katharine thought that too, and she never did get to see her daughter again."

Tj closed her eyes. She could feel herself drifting off.

"You have to stay awake." Kiara gently nudged her.

"I'm just so tired. Maybe if I could sleep for a few minutes..."

"No, you have to stay awake," Kiara insisted. "I'm so sorry this happened to you. We never planned for Papa to find out we were here. Now everything is such a mess."

"How did he know you were here?" Tj wondered.

"I don't know. I didn't tell anyone, not even Annabeth. I knew there could be trouble, so I was very careful."

Tj frowned. "What about Katharine? Do you think she would have told anyone?"

"Katharine only lived in the area for about a year, and Papa kept close tabs on her. I doubt she even knew anyone to tell. It doesn't make any sense that she'd tell Papa or Aaron."

Tj leaned against the wall as she thought about it. It had warmed up a bit. The sun was now at an angle that allowed a streak of sunshine through the window. Tj sat in that small streak while Kiara curled up on the bed. Either Kiara or Katharine had to have mentioned their plans to someone. But who? And why?

"One of the models mentioned that Tonya—or rather, Katharine—had a gambling problem and owed people money. Do you know anything about that?" Tj asked.

"Actually, yeah," Kiara admitted. "It was when we were at the regional competition in Vegas. She got caught up in the gambling frenzy and lost a lot of money. I was really mad. She almost ruined everything. She said she had no idea what came over her and was sorry and wouldn't let it happen again. She was lucky the Tropical Tan people put her on probation instead of firing her."

"Did she ever say anything about being afraid of the people she owed money to?"

"Once, about two or three weeks ago. We met to finalize our plan and she seemed more nervous than usual. I asked what was wrong and she said nothing, but I could tell she was worried about something. I figured she was getting cold feet about trying to sneak off with Annabeth. I asked her if that was it, and she said no, she'd just gotten herself into some trouble and was trying to figure out how to get out of it. She didn't want to talk about it, but one of the other girls told me that she'd seen Tonya talking to a man outside her hotel room a few nights before. According to the model I spoke to, the man was big and scary. She said he had a gun tucked into his pants. I asked Katharine about it the next day and she said she'd handled it and there was nothing to worry about. She left a couple of days after that to come here and make the final arrangements. I didn't see her again until the day in the cove."

Tj couldn't help but wonder if there wasn't more to the story than even Kiara knew. It wouldn't be unreasonable to assume that Katharine was being shaken down for the money she owed to what sounded like less-than-respectable moneylenders. Maybe she'd seen the deal she'd made with Kiara as a way to take care of two problems at the same time, trading Kiara to her father in exchange for her own daughter and cash. Katharine was dead and it didn't serve to sully her memory by bringing up this possibility, but it certainly would explain a lot.

"Shhh, someone's coming," Kiara whispered. She climbed the stairs and looked out of the window. "It's a gorgeous man in a deputy's uniform; he looks madder than I've ever seen anyone look."

"It must be Dylan. Stand back; he'll probably break down the door. He isn't known for his patience when it comes to someone messing with people he cares about."

Tj got up in anticipation of Dylan's arrival. She was about to join Kiara at the door when she heard a pop, pop, pop.

"What happened?" Tj struggled toward the small window.

"Someone shot the deputy."

"Oh God."

Tj tried to see what was happening, but her line of sight was limited to what was directly in front of her. She heard several more shots that seemed to come from every direction at the same time and then nothing.

"Can you see anything?" Tj whispered. Tears were running down her face. If Dylan was dead, it would be all her fault. She should never have come looking for Kiara alone. If she'd waited and called the sheriff's office like she should have, they would have arrived with a plan in place.

"No," Kiara answered. "I can hear someone coming, though."

Both girls stepped toward the back of the room as Dylan came crashing through the door. Tj ran forward and fell into his arms. He picked her up and held her close.

"Are you okay?" he asked.

"Bump on the head, but I'll be fine." Tj couldn't stop the tears that streamed down her face. "Kiara saw you get shot. I thought you were dead."

Dylan kissed her forehead and held her close to his body. She could hear the pounding of his heart. "Bulletproof vest," he explained. "I'll have a hell of a bruise, but I'll live. Are you okay?" He looked at Kiara.

"I'm fine, but we should get out of here. I heard gunfire. Do you know who shot you?"

"A man who I believe is your father."

Kiara paled.

"Don't worry, he's alive. One of the other deputies is taking him down to the sheriff's office. I should get the two of you to the hospital."

"Annabeth…" Tj stopped him.

"She's with Kyle."

"Kyle?" Tj asked.

"I called him after Annabeth called 911 and Roy called me, which is what you should have done in the first place. It was careless of you to look for Kiara by yourself. You could have gotten hurt a lot worse than you did. And you could have been responsible for getting someone else hurt as well."

"I know." Tj wrapped her arms around Dylan's neck and cried harder. "I can't bear the thought of you leaving. I wanted to keep this whole situation as far away from your sister as possible. I thought that if I could rescue Kiara, you wouldn't have to be called away from your leave. Now I've made it worse."

Dylan ran his finger down her cheek and gently kissed her on the lips. The kiss was so soft as to barely be felt, but it was tender and sent shivers down her spine. He looked deeply into her eyes. She sensed his hesitation. Tj knew he regretted the kiss almost before he'd delivered it. She felt her heart break as he emotionally slipped away. She'd messed things up. He knew it and she knew it. His sister would never stay and he would have to go.

"I need to finish up here," Dylan said, an air of detachment in his voice. "Roy will drive you both to the hospital. I've called Hunter and he's waiting there."

"I feel fine. I don't need to go to the hospital," Tj insisted. "Just have someone take me home. I'm sure Grandpa is frantic."

"Your grandfather has been notified, and we both know Hunter is never going to let you get away without being checked out. If you don't go to Hunter, I can assure you he'll come to you. He's been worried. We all have."

"Okay. I'll go. You'll come by later?" Tj didn't want to let him go.

"If I can."

CHAPTER 19

Friday, July 25

Tj walked down Main Street, taking in the festive atmosphere of the summer afternoon. The sun was out and the beach was packed, and when the beach was packed, so were the restaurants and small shops that made up the main part of the colorful little town. Tj paused in front of a rack of bikinis that were showcased to draw window-shoppers into the new sun-and-sand shop that featured everything one would need for a day on the beach. It had been a year since she'd gotten a new suit, and the red and orange bikini hanging at the front of the rack had caught her eye as she walked by.

It had been over a month since Tj and Kiara had been rescued from the cellar in which Annabeth's dad had locked them. She'd been x-rayed, poked, and prodded to the point that she felt she might scream before Hunter had deemed her fit enough to go home. She hated spending two days in the hospital. Even the nurses thought Hunter was being overly cautious. But he had been so sweet and attentive while she was in his care. He spent most of his breaks with her, and sat with her each night until she fell asleep. She'd told him that he was acting like a mother hen, requiring all the tests, but he'd held her oh so sweetly and told her that he would never be able to live with himself if he missed something and she suffered permanent damage due to his error.

After more than a month, Dylan's sister was still in town, so he'd only been by to visit a couple of times, and even then only for a few minutes. Tj understood. Everyone's happiness depended on his sister finding a sense of security in Serenity, and reminding her that her brother had been pulled away from his family to rescue the impulsive woman who everyone knew was his sort-of girlfriend wasn't the image any of them wanted to leave her with.

With their dad in jail, Kiara had been granted temporary custody of her sister. They would need to go to court to make it permanent, but Tj saw no reason why the request wouldn't be granted. Nona testified that Aaron, on the order of Kiara's father, had sent her on a wild-goose chase looking for Kiara. She believed Aaron when he told her that Kiara had notified him that she was in trouble and needed help. Tj supposed that much, at least, was true. The lie came into play when Aaron fed her false leads that had her running from one dead end to another.

Aaron claimed he never wanted to hurt Kiara or lie to Nona. He stated that Katharine approached his father about bringing her to Serenity in exchange for Kiara and enough money to get the thugs off her back. He'd agreed and got Aaron to cooperate by threatening to hurt Kiara if he didn't. The sheriff decided, after much consideration, to charge him with a lesser crime than the two men who had masterminded the whole affair. Aaron was given probation and community service and encouraged to seek employment outside the confines of Vengeance. After obtaining a job at Grainger's General Store, which included a very small studio apartment over the storage area, Aaron made the decision to move into town.

Tj replaced the bikini on the rack and continued down the sidewalk. Children from five to fifty crowded the all-purpose sports trail that ran parallel to the beach as kids on skates, grandmas on bikes, and teens on scooters, made their way from one end of town to the other. Occasionally, Tj brought her inline skates down in the early morning before most of the crowd arrived. She stopped at a cute boutique that sold clothes for the active teen, an adorable outfit in camouflage catching her eye. She'd be willing to bet it was something Annabeth would adore. Introducing Annabeth to the luxury of new clothes was like introducing a moth to a flame. Once Annabeth realized that Kyle was more than happy to buy her whatever she needed, the awkward caterpillar transformed into a beautiful butterfly with an eye for style.

Kiara still very much wanted to go to college, so Kyle was helping her work on a plan that, it seemed, would make her dreams come true, as well as allow her to support both herself and Annabeth in the long run. After it was evident that Annabeth's father was going to jail, Kyle had talked to his mother about making a permanent commitment to the sisters. Kyle's mother was in her element with two "daughters" to dote on and couldn't wait to agree to Kyle's idea.

Kyle found a three-bedroom house in town where his mom could provide housing for both Kiara and Annabeth while the older girl could attend community college in order to get the prerequisites she'd need to apply to a university in a year's time. Annabeth was thrilled to have a mother substitute doting on her, and Kiara was grateful for the help Kyle and his mom insisted on providing. With the girls to focus her energy on, Kyle's mother was meddling in his life much less than she had since she'd arrived, so the tension that had threatened their relationship seemed to have dissipated, at least for the time being.

Tj realized that if she was going to buy an outfit for Annabeth, she should buy one for Ashley and Gracie as well. Her dad and sisters had returned the day after she'd gotten out of the hospital. She was glad she'd spared them the worry they would have had to endure had they been home and fully aware of what was going on.

The models had gone and the resort returned to the families Tj enjoyed. She wouldn't miss the demanding models, but she would miss Chloe, who, to everyone's surprise, had won the contest and would be the next Ms. Tropical Tan. In the days since the event, Chloe and Kiara had talked about applying to the same school next year. Chloe would be finished with her spokesmodel commitment about the same time Kiara would be done with her prerequisites, if all went as planned. Tj was glad that Kiara had found a friend her own age with similar goals and interests.

Annabeth was going to attend public school in the fall. She was a bright girl who, in spite of the fact that she'd had no formal education, didn't seem to be all that far behind. Tj had agreed to tutor her over the remainder of the summer so she'd be ready in September. It warmed Tj's heart to see Annabeth blossom. She was happy and carefree and thrilled with the new life Kyle had provided for her. Amber and Kiara had become fast friends, quickly settling into a routine of shopping, hanging out at the beach, and dating, as girls their age were supposed to do.

Deciding to stop off at the post office while she was in town, Tj returned to her SUV to drop off her packages, then headed on foot toward the county buildings.

The mystery surrounding Fenton Ridley and his son never

did get sorted out. Fenton had told Roy he had proof that Porter had killed Tonya, but after Kiara's father was exposed as the killer, Fenton recanted his statement and Sheriff Boggs let him do so without so much as an explanation. Tj suspected Fenton and Porter had been butting heads since Porter showed up on his doorstep. Perhaps Fenton truly believed Porter was guilty of killing Tonya, or perhaps he simply saw the murder as a way to get his son out of his hair. Either way, the last she'd heard, Porter had been given a promotion and a raise, so apparently Fenton was continuing the tradition he'd established of buying his son's forgiveness.

"Afternoon, Hazel," Tj said as she arrived at the post office.

"Tj, I'm glad you stopped by. You have a certified letter. I was just about to leave you a message."

"A certified letter? For me?"

"Has your name on it," Hazel confirmed. "You'll need to sign right here before I can hand it over. It looks like it's from a law office. I hope there isn't any trouble."

Tj signed where Hazel instructed and looked at the address. It was from a law firm in Los Angeles. Occasionally, someone suffered a slip and fall at the resort and attorneys got involved, but those letters were always addressed to her dad. She couldn't imagine what an attorney in Los Angeles—or anywhere else, for that matter—would want with her.

Tj knew Hazel hoped she'd open the letter right there, but she decided to wait until after she'd left the scrutiny of one of the biggest gossips in town. Taking the pile of mail Hazel handed her, Tj walked out the front door and headed toward a picnic table in the shade, set on a slight hill. It provided a view of the lake while ensuring a modicum of isolation from the hustle and bustle of the sand lining the water.

Tj tore open the letter and began to read. Tears streamed

down her face as she stared blankly at the white parchment. The sound of children's laughter in the background faded as Tj felt her entire world collapse around her.

"Tj."

She looked up to see Dylan standing beside her.

"Are you all right?"

Tj stared at him blankly. She knew she should respond, but somehow she couldn't form words.

"Has something happened?" he asked.

Tj wasn't sure why she didn't step into his arms, but for some reason she didn't understand, she slid the manila envelope under the pile of mail and forced a smile to her face.

"I'm fine," she lied. "I've just had one of those days, and I got a letter that kind of threw me for a loop, but I'm fine."

"I hoped we could talk." Dylan hesitated, as if he realized she might dissolve into a puddle of mush at any moment.

"Have a seat." Tj motioned to the bench next to her. "What's on your mind?"

"My sister and I had a long talk last night."

Tj's heart began to pound. She knew that everything she'd shared with Dylan, everything she hoped to share in the future, had come down to this instant.

"And?" Tj could barely whisper the word.

Dylan paused. He looked Tj directly in the eye. "Are you sure you want to do this now?"

Tj nodded. The tears she'd unsuccessfully tried to control slid down her cheek. If his news was good, he'd come right out with it.

"The good news is that Allie has admitted it's best for Justin if I'm an everyday part of his life. He needs a man to help guide him." Dylan looked directly at Tj. "He needs me."

"I know," Tj whispered.

"Although Allie has agreed that I'm a vital part of Justin's life, she confessed that, try as she might, she just isn't comfortable with my being an officer of the law. I don't know if she can ever get over what happened to Anna, what almost happened to me, and what could have happened to Justin if he'd been at our apartment on the day of the shooting."

"You're quitting your job?"

"I handed in my resignation this morning."

"You're going back to Chicago?" Tj was certain she knew the answer but had to ask anyway.

"No, we aren't going to live in Chicago."

Tj felt hope, only to have it dashed within seconds.

"I've taken a job with a home and business security software firm in San Francisco. I have an appointment to list my house this evening." Dylan looked longingly into her eyes. "We plan to be fully relocated before school starts in the fall."

Tj bit her lip and tried to suppress the tears that refused to be quelled.

"I'm so sorry." Dylan could no longer hide the grief on his face. "I really care about you. I'd hoped we'd have a chance to see where our relationship might go, but this is something I have to do."

"I understand," Tj said, and she did. Maybe more now than ever. When it came to relationships, the children in your life always had to come first. Tj wanted to say something more, but there were no words to convey her emotions. She watched as Dylan stepped back and waved at someone behind her.

"I have to go." He leaned forward, kissed her soundly on the lips, and walked away.

Hunter sat down next to her. She wrapped her arms around his neck and wept. Hunter held her, whispering words of support, until all her tears were spent.

"What are you doing here?" Tj finally looked up and asked.

"Dylan called me," Hunter admitted. "I think I'm your consolation prize."

Tj laughed. She wiped away the tears that had wet her face. "Consolation prize?"

"Dylan saw you sitting here from his office window. He knew what he needed to do and figured this was as good a time as any to do it. He didn't want you to be alone, so he called me to ask if I could come over. I was at the hospital, so I agreed. If he had stayed, I'm sure he would have fought for you, but since he had to leave, I think that having me show up was his way of giving you to me."

"Giving me to you?"

"Symbolically."

Tj rolled her eyes.

"He cares about you," Hunter pointed out.

"I know. I care about him too."

"What do you think?" Hunter spread his arms, presenting himself. "Do I make an acceptable consolation prize?"

Tj laughed while tears began to fall again. She cupped Hunter's cheek and looked directly into his eyes. "You're much more than a consolation prize."

Hunter smiled, a look of sadness on his face. "But not the grand prize either?"

Tj sighed. "I don't know. I love you. I've always loved you and will always love you. But honestly..."

"Yeah." Hunter squeezed her hand. "I know. We had our time."

"We did. And maybe we'll have another time. Who knows what the future holds, but for now, I think I need to remain attachment-free until I can figure things out. Things have suddenly become really, really confusing."

Hunter put his arm around her. "Can I help?"

Tj handed him the certified letter. He opened it and began to read.

"Tj!" Gracie came running up as Hunter made his way through the document. She catapulted herself into Tj's arms and gave her a sloppy kiss. Ashley, Kristi, and Kari were doing cartwheels across the lawn, with Jenna trailing behind.

Jenna had taken all four girls to a movie and then the arcade. It had been a full day and her little family couldn't wait to tell her about it.

"Look what I got you." Gracie proudly handed Tj a small stuffed dog. "I won it all by myself."

"You did?" Tj smiled. "I love it. It's the best present anyone ever gave me." She hugged Gracie with all her might.

"You can put it on your bed," Gracie said.

"I'll definitely put it on my bed."

"His name is Sebastian," Gracie informed her.

"Sebastian is the most perfect stuffed doggy name I've ever heard."

"We're going to get ice cream. Do you want to come?"

"More than anything." Tj boosted Gracie into position as she wrapped her legs around Tj's waist and her arms around her neck. Tj held her close and breathed in the scent of her recently washed hair. It had been a difficult day, but Tj found comfort in Gracie's embrace as the others began talking all at once.

She glanced at Hunter, who gave her a look that assured her that whatever happened in the future, he'd be there for her. He tucked the letter back into the envelope and returned it to the stack of mail as Ashley told Tj about the movie and the cute fourth-grade boy who'd sat in the row just in front of them. Hunter stood up and gave Tj a quick but firm hug before transferring Gracie to his back.

Tj took Ashley's hand as the group headed toward the beach and the ice cream truck. She rested her head on Hunter's arm and watched the day come to a close. As the sun set behind the distant mountain, she took comfort in her firm belief that at the end of the day, righteousness prevailed and love conquered all.

KATHI DALEY

Kathi Daley lives with her husband, kids, grandkids, and Bernese mountain dogs in beautiful Lake Tahoe. When she isn't writing, she likes to read (preferably at the beach or by the fire), cook (preferably something with chocolate or cheese), and garden (planting and planning, not weeding). She also enjoys spending time in the water, hiking, biking, and snowshoeing. Kathi uses the mountain setting in which she lives, along with the animals (wild and domestic) that share her home, as inspiration for her five cozy mystery series: Zoe Donovan, Whales and Tails Island, Tj Jensen, Sand and Sea Hawaiian, and Seacliff High Teen.

**The Tj Jensen Mystery Series
by Kathi Daley**

Henery Press Mystery Books

And finally, before you go...
Here are a few other mysteries
you might enjoy:

THE SEMESTER OF OUR DISCONTENT

Cynthia Kuhn

A Lila Maclean Mystery (#1)

English professor Lila Maclean is thrilled about her new job at prestigious Stonedale University, until she finds one of her colleagues dead. She soon learns that everyone, from the chancellor to the detective working the case, believes Lila—or someone she is protecting—may be responsible for the horrific event, so she assigns herself the task of identifying the killer.

More attacks on professors follow, the only connection a curious symbol at each of the crime scenes. Putting her scholarly skills to the test, Lila gathers evidence, but her search is complicated by an unexpected nemesis, a suspicious investigator, and an ominous secret society. Rather than earning an "A" for effort, she receives a threat featuring the mysterious emblem and must act quickly to avoid failing her assignment...and becoming the next victim.

Available at booksellers nationwide and online

Visit www.henerypress.com for details

COUNTERFEIT CONSPIRACIES

Ritter Ames

A Bodies of Art Mystery (#1)

Laurel Beacham may have been born with a silver spoon in her mouth, but she has long since lost it digging herself out of trouble. Her father gambled and womanized his way through the family fortune before skiing off an Alp, leaving her with more tarnish than trust fund. Quick wits and connections have gained her a reputation as one of the world's premier art recovery experts. The police may catch the thief, but she reclaims the missing masterpieces.

The latest assignment, however, may be her undoing. Using every ounce of luck and larceny she possesses, Laurel must locate a priceless art icon and rescue a co-worker (and ex-lover) from a master criminal, all the while matching wits with a charming new nemesis. Unfortunately, he seems to know where the bodies are buried—and she prefers hers isn't next.

Available at booksellers nationwide and online

Visit www.henerypress.com for details

ARTIFACT

Gigi Pandian

A Jaya Jones Treasure Hunt Mystery (#1)

Historian Jaya Jones discovers the secrets of a lost Indian treasure may be hidden in a Scottish legend from the days of the British Raj. But she's not the only one on the trail...

From San Francisco to London to the Highlands of Scotland, Jaya must evade a shadowy stalker as she follows hints from the hastily scrawled note of her dead lover to a remote archaeological dig. Helping her decipher the cryptic clues are her magician best friend, a devastatingly handsome art historian with something to hide, and a charming archaeologist running for his life.

Available at booksellers nationwide and online

Visit www.henerypress.com for details